When We Cease to
Understand the World

When We Cease to Understand the World

BENJAMÍN LABATUT

Translated from the Spanish by Adrian Nathan West

nyrb **New York Review Books** New York

This is a New York Review Book

published by The New York Review of Books

207 East 32nd Street, New York, NY 10016

www.nyrb.com

LIBRARY OF CONGRESS CATALOGING-IN-PUBLICATION DATA
Names: Labatut, Benjamín, 1980– author. | West, Adrian Nathan, translator.
Title: When we cease to understand the world / Benjamin Labatut ; translated
by Adrian Nathan West.
Other titles: Verdor terrible. English
Description: New York : New York Review Books, [2021]
Identifiers: LCCN 2021005101 (print) | LCCN 2021005102 (ebook) |
ISBN 9781681375663 (paperback) | ISBN 9781681375670 (ebook)
Subjects: LCSH: Labatut, Benjamín, 1980– —Translations into English. |
Scientists—Fiction. | LCGFT: Short stories.
Classification: LCC PQ8098.422.A215 V4713 2021 (print) | LCC
PQ8098.422.A215 (ebook) | DDC 863/.7--dc23
LC record available at https://lccn.loc.gov/2021005101
LC ebook record available at https://lccn.loc.gov/2021005102

ISBN 978-1-68137-566-3
Available as an electronic book; ISBN 978-1-68137-567-0

Printed in the United States of America on acid-free paper

20 19 18

Contents

Prussian Blue

In a medical examination on the eve of the Nuremberg Trials, the doctors found the nails of Hermann Göring's fingers and toes stained a furious red, the consequence of his addiction to dihydrocodeine, an analgesic of which he took more than one hundred pills a day. William Burroughs described it as similar to heroin, twice as strong as codeine, but with a wired coke-like edge, so the North American doctors felt obliged to cure Göring of his dependency before allowing him to stand before the court. This was not easy. When the Allied forces caught him, the Nazi leader was dragging a suitcase with more than twenty thousand doses, practically all that remained of Germany's production of the drug at the end of the Second World War. His addiction was far from exceptional, for virtually everyone in the Wehrmacht received Pervitin as part of their rations, methamphetamine tablets that the troopers used to stay awake for weeks on end, fighting in a deranged state, alternating between manic furore and nightmarish stupor, with overexertion leading many to suffer attacks of irrepressible euphoria. "An absolute silence reigns. Everything becomes alien and insignificant. I feel completely weightless, as if I were floating above my own airplane," a Luftwaffe pilot wrote years later, as though he were recollecting the silent raptures of a beatific vision rather than the dog days of war. The German writer Heinrich

Böll wrote letters to his family from the front asking them to send him additional doses: "It's hard here," he wrote to his parents on November 9, 1939, "and I hope you understand if I can only write you every two or three days. Today I'm doing so chiefly to ask for more Pervitin . . . I love you, Hein." On May 20, 1940, he wrote them a long, impassioned letter that ended with the same request: "Can you get hold of a bit more Pervitin for me, so I can have some in reserve?" Two months later, his parents received a single scraggly line: "If at all possible, please mail me more Pervitin." Amphetamines fuelled the unrelenting German Blitzkrieg and many soldiers suffered psychotic attacks as they felt the bitter tablets dissolve on their tongues. The Reich leadership, however, tasted something very different when the lightning war was extinguished by the firestorms of the Allied bombers, when the Russian winter froze the caterpillar tracks of their tanks and the Führer ordered everything of value within the Reich destroyed to leave nothing but scorched earth for the invading troops. Faced with utter defeat, staggered by the new horror they had called down upon the world, they chose a quick escape, biting down on cyanide capsules and choking to death on the sweet scent of almonds that the poison gives off.

A wave of suicides swept through Germany in the final months of the war. In April 1945 alone, three thousand eight hundred people killed themselves in Berlin. The inhabitants of the small town of Demmin, to the north of the capital, some three hours away, fell prey to collective panic when the retreating German troops destroyed the bridges leading west, leaving them stranded on their peninsula, surrounded by three rivers and defenceless before the dreaded onslaught of the Red Army. Hundreds of men, women and children took their own lives over the course of three days. Whole families walked into the waters of the Tollense tied together with ropes around their waists, as if to play a gruesome game of tug of war, the smallest children weighed down by their schoolbags, laden with rocks. The chaos was such that the Russian troops—who had, up to then, devoted themselves to looting homes, burning buildings and raping women—received orders to put a stop to the epidemic of suicides; on three separate occasions they had to cut down a woman who tried to hang herself from the branches of a massive oak tree in her garden, at the roots of which she had already buried her three children, after lacing their cookies—a final treat—with rat poison. The woman survived, but the soldiers were unable to prevent a young girl from bleeding to death after she opened her veins with the same razor blade she had used to slice her parents' wrists. A similar death wish took hold of the upper echelons of the Nazi party: fifty-three generals from the army, fourteen from the air force, and eleven from the navy committed suicide, along with the Minister of Education, Bernhard Rust, the Minister of Justice, Otto Thierack, Field Marshal Walter Model, the "Desert Fox" Erwin Rommel and, of course, the Führer himself. Others, such as Hermann Göring, hesitated and were captured alive, but this merely postponed the inevitable. When the doctors declared him fit for trial, Göring was found guilty by the Nuremberg Tribunal and condemned to death by hanging. He requested a firing squad: he wished to die like a soldier and not a common criminal. When he learned of the refusal of this last request, he killed himself by biting on a cyanide capsule he had hidden in a jar of pomade next to which he left a note explaining that he had chosen to die by his own hand, "like the great Hannibal". The Allies attempted to wipe away all traces of his existence. They removed the shards of glass from his lips and sent his clothing, personal effects and naked body to the municipal crematorium at the Ostfriedhof cemetery in Munich, where one of the gigantic ovens was fired up to incinerate Göring, mingling his ashes with those of thousands of political prisoners and opponents of the Nazi regime decapitated at Stadelheim prison, the handicapped children and psychiatric patients murdered by the Aktion T4 euthanasia programme, and countless victims of the concentration camp system. His remains were scattered late at night in the waters of the Watzenbach, a small brook chosen from a map at random. But these efforts were in vain: to this day, collectors from all over the world continue to exchange keepsakes and belongings of the last great leader of the Nazis, commander of the Luftwaffe and Hitler's natural successor. In June 2016, an Argentine man paid more than three thousand euros for a pair of the Reichsmarschall's silk underpants. Months later, that same man spent twenty-six thousand euros on the copper and zinc cylinder that had once concealed the glass vial Göring ground between his teeth on October 15, 1946.

The National Socialist party elite received similar capsules at the end of the last concert given by the Berlin Philharmonic before the city fell on April 12, 1945. Albert Speer, Minister of Armaments and War Production and official architect of the Third Reich, organized a special programme that included Beethoven's Violin Concerto in D major, followed by Brückner's Fourth Symphony—*The Romantic*—and ending, appropriately, with Brünnhilde's aria, which closes the third act of Richard Wagner's *Götterdämmerung*, in which the Valkyrie immolates herself on an enormous funeral pyre, the flames of which spread to consume not only the world of men but the halls of Valhalla and the entire pantheon of the gods. When the audience filed towards the exits, Brünnhilde's cries of pain still resounding in their ears, members of the Deutsches Jungvolk—a section of the Hitler Youth composed of children under ten, as the teenagers were already off dying at the barricades—handed out cyanide capsules in small wicker baskets, like votive offerings at mass. Göring, Goebbels, Bormann and Himmler used these capsules to commit suicide, but many of the Nazi leaders chose to shoot themselves in the head at the same moment they bit down, afraid that they had been sabotaged, that the capsules were deliberately adulterated to provoke not the painless, instant death that they desired but the slow agony they deserved. Hitler became so convinced that his dosage had been tampered with that he chose to test its effectiveness on his beloved Blondi, a German shepherd that had accompanied him to the Führerbunker, where she slept at the foot of his bed, enjoying privileges of all kinds. The Führer preferred killing his pet to letting her fall into the hands of Russian troops who had already surrounded Berlin and were inching closer to his subterranean refuge by the minute, but he was too cowardly to do it himself; he asked his personal doctor to break one of the capsules in the animal's mouth. The dog— who had just given birth to four puppies—died instantly when the minuscule cyanide molecule, formed by one atom of nitrogen, one of carbon and one of potassium, entered her bloodstream and cut off her breath.

The effects of cyanide are so swift that there is but one historical account of its flavour, left behind in the early twenty-first century by M.P. Prasad, an Indian goldsmith, thirty-two years old, who managed to write three lines after swallowing it: "Doctors, potassium cyanide. I have tasted it. It burns the tongue and tastes acrid," said the note found next to his body in the hotel room he had rented for the purpose of taking his own life. The liquid form of the poison, known in Germany as *Blausäure* or blue acid, is highly volatile: it boils at twenty-six degrees Celsius and gives off a slight aroma of almonds, which not everyone can distinguish, as doing so requires a gene absent in forty per cent of humanity. This evolutionary caprice makes it likely that a significant number of the Jews murdered with Zyklon B in Auschwitz-Birkenau, Majdanek and Mauthausen did not even notice the scent of cyanide filling the gas chambers, while others died smelling the same fragrance inhaled by the men who had organized their extermination as they bit down on their suicide capsules.

Decades before, Zyklon A—a precursor to the poison employed by the Nazis in their concentration camps—had been sprayed on California oranges, as a pesticide, and used to delouse the trains in which tens of thousands of Mexican immigrants hid when entering the United States. The wood of the train cars was stained a beautiful blue, the same colour that can be seen even today on certain bricks at Auschwitz; both hearken to cyanide's authentic origins as a by-product isolated in 1782 from the first modern synthetic pigment, Prussian Blue.

As soon as it appeared, Prussian Blue caused a sensation in European art. Thanks to its lower price, in just a few years it had all but replaced the colour that painters had used since the Renaissance to depict the robes of the angels and the Virgin's mantle—ultramarine, the finest and costliest of all blue pigments, which was obtained by grinding lapis lazuli brought up from caves in Afghanistan's Kochka river valley.

Crushed to a fine powder, this mineral yielded a lavish indigo, which proved impossible to emulate by chemical means until the eighteenth century, when a Swiss pigmenter and dyer by the name of Johann Jacob Diesbach discovered Prussian Blue. He did so by accident: his aim had been to mimic the ruby red made by crushing millions of female cochineals, small parasitic insects that grow on the nopal cactus in Mexico and in Central and South America, creatures so fragile that they require even greater care than silkworms, since wind, rain and frost can easily damage their downy white bodies, while rats, birds and caterpillars continually prey on them. Their scarlet blood—along with silver and gold—was one of the greatest treasures the Spanish conquistadors stole from the American peoples, and it allowed the Spanish crown to establish a monopoly on carmine that would last for centuries. Diesbach tried to put an end to it by pouring *sale tartari* (potash) over a distillation of animal parts mixed by one of his apprentices, the young alchemist Johann Conrad Dippel; but the concoction, instead of producing the furious carmine of the *Dactylopius coccus*, yielded a blue of such beauty that Diesbach thought he had discovered *hsbd-iryt*, the original colour of the sky— the legendary blue used by the Egyptians to adorn the skin of their gods. Passed down across the centuries, closely guarded by the priests of Egypt as part of their divine covenant, its formula was stolen by a Greek thief and lost forever after the fall of the Roman Empire. Diesbach dubbed his new colour "Prussian Blue" to establish an intimate and long-lasting connection between his chance discovery and the empire that would surpass the glory of the ancients, as it would have taken a much more gifted man—one endowed, perhaps, with the curse of foresight—even to conceive of its future fall. Diesbach lacked not only this sublime imagination, but even the most basic skills of commerce and enterprise needed to enjoy the material benefits of his creation, which fell, instead, into the hands of his financier, the ornithologist, linguist and entomologist Johann Leonhard Frisch, who turned his blue into gold.

Frisch amassed a fortune as a wholesaler of Prussian Blue to shops in Paris, London and St Petersburg. He used his profits to buy hundreds of hectares near Spandau, where he established the first silk plantation in Prussia. A passionate naturalist, Frisch wrote a long letter to the emperor exalting the singular virtues of the tiny silkworm; the letter also described an ambitious, transformative agricultural undertaking, an idea that had come to him in a dream: he had seen mulberry trees growing in the courtyards of all the churches of the empire, their verdant leaves feeding the offspring of the *Bombyx mori*. The plan, timidly put into practice by Frederick the Great, was taken up with violence one hundred and fifty years later by the Third Reich. The Nazis planted millions of such trees in abandoned fields and residential quarters, in schoolyards and cemeteries, in the grounds of hospitals and sanatoria, and on both sides of the highways that criss-crossed the new Germany. They distributed guides and manuals of all kinds to small farmers, detailing the state-sanctioned techniques for the harvesting and processing of silkworms: they were to be suspended over a vessel of boiling water for more than three hours, the minimum time required to kill them without damaging the precious material of the cocoons they had woven around themselves. Frisch himself included this procedure in an appendix to his magnum opus, an eighteen-tome work to which he dedicated the last twenty years of his life; these books catalogue, with a scrupulousness bordering on madness, the three hundred species of insect native to Germany. The final volume details the complete life cycle of the field cricket, from its nymph stage to the courtship songs of the males, a chirrup as shrill and piercing as the whistle of a train. Frisch describes this along with their reproductive habits and the oviposition of the females, the eggs of which are surprisingly similar in colour to the pigment that had made him a wealthy man, and which artists across Europe adopted as soon as it became commercially available.

The first great painter to make use of it was the Dutchman Pieter van der Werff, in 1709: in his portrayal of *The Entombment of Christ* clouds mask the horizon, and the blue cloak that darkens the Virgin's face shimmers, reflecting the grief of the disciples who surround the naked corpse of the Messiah, his skin so pallid it illuminates the face of the woman kneeling to kiss the back of his hand, as though wishing to cauterize with her lips the wounds opened by the iron nails.

Iron, gold, silver, copper, tin, lead, phosphorus, arsenic; at the beginning of the eighteenth century, mankind was aware of only a handful of pure elements. Chemistry had not yet branched away from alchemy, and the compounds known by a myriad of arcane names such as bismuth, vitriol, cinnabar and amalgam were a hatchery for unexpected, often happy accidents. Prussian Blue, for example, would never have existed were it not for the young alchemist working in the pigmentary where the colour was first synthesized. Johann Conrad Dippel presented himself as a Pietist theologian, a philosopher, artist and doctor; his detractors thought him a simple quack. He was born in the small Frankenstein Castle near Darmstadt, and possessed from childhood a strange charisma that affected anyone who spent too much time in his presence. He even took in, for a time, one of the great scientific minds of his era, the Swedish mystic Emanuel Swedenborg, who became one of his most enthusiastic disciples, and later his sworn enemy. According to Swedenborg, Dippel had the gift of dispossessing people of their faith and depriving them of all intelligence and goodwill. He would entice his followers with promises of apotheosis only to "abandon them in a state of delirium". In one of his most impassioned diatribes, Swedenborg likens him to Satan himself: "He is the wickedest of demons, bound by no principle, indeed, generally opposed to all of them." His criticisms had no effect on Dippel, who was immune to scandal after spending seven years in prison for his heretical ideas and practices. His sentence served, he renounced all pretence to humanity, and engaged in countless experiments on live and dead animals, which he dissected with unnatural fervour. His aim was to enter history as the first man to transplant a soul from one body to another, but, in the end, he became infamous for his extreme cruelty and the perverse joy he took in manipulating the remains of his victims. In his work *Maladies and Remedies of the Life of the Flesh*, published in Leiden under the pseudonym Christianus Democritus, he claimed to have discovered the Elixir of Life—a liquid counterpart to the Philosopher's Stone—which would heal any ailment and grant eternal life to the person who drank it. He tried, but failed, to exchange the formula for the deed to Frankenstein Castle, and the only use he ever made of his potion—a mixture of decomposing blood, bones, antlers, horns and hooves—was as an insecticide, due to its incomparable stench. This same quality led the German troops to employ the tarry, viscous fluid as a non-lethal chemical weapon (therefore exempt from the Geneva Convention), pouring it into wells in North Africa to slow the advance of General Patton and his men, whose tanks pursued them across the desert sands. An ingredient in Dippel's elixir would eventually produce the blue that shines not only in Van Gogh's *Starry Night* and in the waters of Hokusai's *Great Wave*, but also on the uniforms of the infantrymen of the Prussian army, as though something in the colour's chemical structure invoked violence: a fault, a shadow, an existential stain passed down from those experiments in which the alchemist dismembered living animals to create it, assembling their broken bodies in dreadful chimeras he tried to reanimate with electrical charges, the very same monsters that inspired Mary Shelley to write her masterpiece, *Frankenstein; or, The Modern Prometheus*, in whose pages she warned of the risk of the blind advancement of science, to her the most dangerous of all human arts.

The chemist who discovered cyanide experienced this danger first-hand: in 1782, Carl Wilhelm Scheele stirred a pot of Prussian Blue with a spoon coated in traces of sulphuric acid and created the most potent poison of the modern era. He named this new compound "Prussic acid" and was immediately aware of the enormous potential of its hyperreactivity. What he could not imagine was that two hundred years after his death, well into the twenty-first century, its industrial, medical and chemical applications would be such that, each month, a sufficient quantity would be manufactured to poison every person on the planet. A genius unjustly forgotten, Scheele endured bad luck his entire life: the chemist with the most discoveries of natural elements to his name (seven, including oxygen, which he called "fire air"), he invariably shared credit for each of his finds with less talented scientific colleagues who anticipated him in making their conclusions public. Scheele's publisher waited more than five years to release the book the Swede had prepared with such love and extraordinary rigour that he went so far as to smell and even taste the new substances he had conjured in his laboratory. Scheele was wise enough not to do so with his Prussic acid, which would have killed him in seconds; still, his bad habit cost him his life at age forty-three. He died with a ravaged liver, his body covered head to toe in purulent blisters, paralysed by the build-up of fluid in his joints. These were the same symptoms suffered by thousands of European children whose toys were painted with an arsenic-based pigment Scheele manufactured, unaware of its toxicity: an emerald green so dazzling and seductive it became Napoleon's favourite colour.

Scheele's green covered the wallpaper of the chambers and bathrooms of Longwood, the dark, damp, rat- and spider-infested residence of the Emperor during his six years of imprisonment by the British on the island of St Helena. The toxins in the paint adorning his chambers may explain the high levels of arsenic detected in samples of his hair analysed two centuries after his death, a possible cause of the cancer that ate a hole in his stomach the size of a tennis ball. In the Emperor's final weeks, the illness devastated his body with the same ruthlessness with which his soldiers had laid waste to Europe: his skin took on a cadaverous grey tone, his eyes lost their brilliance and sank into their sockets, his wispy beard was dotted with scraps of food left behind after his fits of vomiting. His arms shed their musculature, and small scabs covered his legs, as though, all of a sudden, they recollected every tiny cut or scratch they had borne through the course of his life. But Napoleon was not the lone sufferer of his exile on the island: the host of servants imprisoned with him at Longwood left numerous records of their constant diarrhoea and stomach aches, the painful swelling of their limbs, and a thirst that no liquid could quench. Several died with symptoms similar to those of the man they had served, but this did not prevent the doctors, gardeners and other members of the staff from fighting over the dead emperor's sheets, unmindful of the bloodstains, streaks of shit and blotches of urine that marred them, and of their almost certain contamination with the substance that had slowly poisoned him.

If arsenic is a patient assassin, hiding out in the most recondite of the body's tissues and accumulating there for years, cyanide takes your breath away. In sufficient concentrations, it stimulates the carotid body's receptors all at once, triggering a reflex that cuts off respiration. Medical literature calls this *the audible gasp* that precedes tachycardia, apnoea, convulsions and cardiovascular collapse. The speed with which it acts made it a favourite of countless assassins: the enemies of Grigori Rasputin, for example, hoped to free Alexandra Feodorovna Romanova, the last tsarina of the Russian Empire, from the cleric's spell by poisoning him with petits fours laced with the poison, but for reasons still unknown, Rasputin was immune. To kill him, they had to shoot him three times in the chest and once in the head, wrap his body with iron chains, and throw it into the frozen waters of the Neva. The failed poisoning only added to the mad monk's fame and the devotion the empress and her four daughters felt for his body, which they ordered their most faithful servants to retrieve from the ice and to place on an altar in the middle of the woods, where it remained, perfectly preserved by the cold, until the authorities chose to incinerate it, this being the only way of ensuring its complete disappearance.

Cyanide proved seductive not only for murderers; after he had grown breasts as a side effect of the chemical castration forced on him by the British government in punishment for his homosexuality, Alan Turing, the genius mathematician and father of computing, killed himself by biting into an apple injected with cyanide. Legend says he did so to imitate a scene from his favourite film, *Snow White*, the couplets of which—*Dip the apple in the brew / Let the sleeping death seep through*—he used to chant to himself while he worked. But the apple was never examined to confirm the hypothesis of suicide (even if the seeds do contain a natural form of it, with only half a cup of them sufficient to kill a human being), and some believe Turing was assassinated by the British secret services, despite his heading the team that broke the code the Germans used to encrypt their communications during the Second World War—a decisive factor in the Allied victory. One of his biographers suggests the ambiguous circumstances of his death (the presence of a flask of cyanide in the room he used as a laboratory, and the handwritten note found next to his bed, containing nothing apart from a list of items to be purchased the next day) were planned by Turing himself, so his mother would believe he had died by accident and would not have to bear the weight of his suicide. This would have been the final eccentricity of a man who brought a unique, personal perspective to each of life's particularities. It bothered him that his office-mates used his favourite mug, so he chained it to a radiator with a padlock; it hangs there to this very day. In 1940, when all of Britain supposed the Germans were soon to invade, Turing

used his savings to buy two enormous silver ingots and buried
them in a forest close to his work. He drew up an elaborate
coded map to recall their location, but hid them so well that
he could not fi nd them at the war's end, even with the aid of
a metal detector. In his free time, he liked to play "Desert
Island", a game that consisted in crafting for himself the
largest possible variety of household products: he made his
own detergent, soap and an insecticide so potent it decimated
his neighbours' gardens. During the war, he rode to his office
in the Cypher School in Bletchley Park on a bicycle with a
defective chain that he refused to repair. Rather than taking
it to the workshop, he would calculate the number of
revolutions the chain could withstand, and would jump off
and adjust it seconds before it came loose. In spring, when
his allergy to pollen became unbearable, he would cover his
face with a gas mask (the British government had distributed
them throughout the population at the start of the war),
sowing panic among those who saw him pass and imagined
an attack was imminent.

That Germany would bomb the island with poison gas
seemed inevitable in that era. An adviser to the British
government estimated that an attack of that kind would
cause more than 250 thousand civilian deaths in the first
week alone, and even newborn infants received their own
specially designed gas masks. Schoolchildren used the
Mickey Mouse model: this grotesque nickname attempted
to mitigate the horror the little ones felt upon hearing
the wooden rattle calling them to cinch the rubber straps
around their heads and breathe through the stinking rubber
on their faces while they followed the instructions from the
Ministry of Home Safety:

Hold your breath.

Hold mask in front of face, with thumbs inside straps.

Thrust chin well forward into mask, pull straps over head as far as they will go.

Run finger round face-piece taking care head-straps are not twisted.

The gas bombs never fell on England, and the children learned that blowing out while wearing their masks sounded like a flurry of farts, but the horror experienced by the soldiers who survived attacks with sarin, mustard and chlorine gas in the trenches in the First World War had seeped into the subconscious of an entire generation. The greatest testament to the terror caused by history's first weapon of mass destruction was the universal acceptance of the prohibition on gas during the Second World War. The North Americans had enormous reserves ready for deployment, and the British had experimented with anthrax on a remote Scottish island, massacring flocks of sheep and goats. Even Hitler, who showed no qualms when using gas in the extermination camps, refused to do so in fields of war, for although his scientists had manufactured some seven thousand tons of sarin, enough to eradicate the population of thirty cities the size of Paris, he had witnessed its effects first-hand as a foot soldier in the trenches of the First World War, had seen the agony of the dying and had suffered some of its lesser effects himself.

The first gas attack in history overwhelmed the French troops entrenched near the small town of Ypres, in Belgium. When they awoke on the morning of Thursday, April 22, 1915, the soldiers saw an enormous greenish cloud creeping towards them across no-man's-land. Twice as high as a man and as dense as winter fog, it stretched from one end of the horizon to the other, as far as the eye could see. The leaves withered on the trees as it passed, birds fell dead from the sky; it tinged the pastureland a sickly metallic colour. A scent like pineapple and bleach filled the throats of the soldiers when the gas reacted with the mucus in their lungs, forming hydrochloric acid. As the cloud pooled in the trenches, hundreds of men fell to the ground convulsing, choking on their own phlegm, yellow mucus bubbling in their mouths, their skin turning blue from lack of oxygen. "The weatherman was right. It was a beautiful day, the sun was shining. Where there was grass, it was blazing green. We should have been going on a picnic, not doing what we were going to do," wrote Willi Siebert, one of the soldiers who opened the six thousand canisters of chlorine gas the Germans released that morning at Ypres. "We suddenly heard the French yelling. In less than a minute they started with the most rifle and machine gun fire that I had ever heard. Every field artillery gun, every machine gun, every rifle that the French possessed must have been firing. I had never heard such a noise. The hail of bullets going over our heads was unbelievable, but it was not stopping the gas. The wind kept moving the gas towards the French lines. We heard the cows bawling and the horses screaming. The French kept on shooting. They couldn't possibly see what they were shooting at. In about fifteen minutes the gunfire petered out. After half an hour, only occasional shots. Then everything was quiet again. In a while it had cleared and we walked past the empty gas bottles. What we saw was total death. Nothing was alive. All of the animals had come out of their holes to die. Dead rabbits, moles, rats and mice were everywhere. The smell of the gas was still in the air. It hung on the few bushes which were left. When we got to the French lines the trenches were empty but in a half mile the bodies of French soldiers were everywhere. It was unbelievable. Then we saw there were some English. You could see where men had clawed at their faces, and throats, trying to breathe. Some had shot themselves. The horses, still in the stables, cows, chickens, everything, all were dead. Everything, even the insects were dead."

The attack at Ypres was overseen by the father of this new method of war, the Jewish chemist Fritz Haber. Haber was a man of genius, and the only one, perhaps, capable of understanding the complex molecular reactions that would blacken the skin of the five thousand soldiers who died at Ypres. His mission's success earned him a promotion to head of the Chemistry section of the Ministry of War and a dinner with Kaiser Wilhelm II himself; but when he returned to Berlin, he had to face his wife's fury. Clara Immerwahr—the first woman to receive a doctorate in chemistry at a German university—had not only seen the effects of the gas on animals in the laboratory; she had also nearly lost her husband when the wind suddenly changed direction during one of his field tests. The gas blew straight towards the hill where Haber was directing his troops on horseback. Haber saved himself, miraculously, but one of his students failed to escape the toxic cloud; Clara watched him die on the ground, writhing as if set upon by an army of ravenous ants. When Haber returned victorious from the massacre at Ypres, Clara accused him of perverting science by devising a method for exterminating human beings on an industrial scale. Haber ignored her: for him, war was war and death was death, regardless of the means of its infliction. He used his two days' furlough to invite his friends to a party that lasted until dawn, and, at its end, his wife walked down to the garden, took off her shoes, and shot herself in the chest with her husband's service revolver. She bled to death in the arms of their thirteen-year-old son, who had run downstairs when he heard the shot. Still in shock, Fritz Haber had to travel the following day to oversee a gas attack on the eastern front. Throughout the war, he went on refining techniques for releasing the gas more efficiently, all the while haunted by his wife's ghost. "It really does me good, every few days, to be at the front, where the bullets fly. There, the only thing that counts is the moment, and one's sole duty is whatever one can do within the confines of the trenches. But then it's back to command headquarters, chained to the telephone, and I hear in my heart the words that the poor woman once said, and, in a vision born of weariness, I see her head emerging from between the orders and the telegrams, and I suffer."

After the 1918 armistice, Fritz Haber was declared a war criminal by the Allies, though they were no less keen in their use of gas than the Central Powers. He was forced to flee Germany, and he took up residence in Switzerland, where he received notice that he had won the Nobel Prize for Chemistry for a discovery he had made not long before the war, one that would alter the destiny of the human race in the coming decades.

In 1907, Haber was the first to obtain nitrogen, the main nutrient required for plant growth, directly from the air. In this way, from one day to the next, he addressed the scarcity of fertilizer that threatened to unleash an unprecedented global famine at the beginning of the twentieth century. Had it not been for Haber, hundreds of millions of people who until then had depended on natural fertilizers such as guano and saltpetre for their crops would have died from lack of nourishment. In prior centuries, Europe's insatiable hunger had driven bands of Englishmen as far as Egypt to despoil the tombs of the ancient pharaohs, in search not of gold, jewels or antiquities, but of the nitrogen contained in the bones of the thousands of slaves buried along with the Nile pharaohs, as sacrificial victims, to serve them even after their deaths. The English tomb raiders had exhausted the reserves in continental Europe; they dug up more than three million human skeletons, along with the bones of hundreds of thousands of dead horses that soldiers had ridden in the battles of Austerlitz, Leipzig and Waterloo, sending them by ship to the port of Hull in the north of England, where they were ground in the bone mills of Yorkshire to fertilize the verdant fields of Albion. On the other side of the Atlantic, the craniums of more than thirty million bison slaughtered on the plains were scavenged by poor Native Americans and peasant farmers, picked up one by one and sold to the Northwestern Bone Syndicate of North Dakota, which stacked them into a pile the size of a church before sending them to the carbon works that ground them to produce fertilizer and "bone black", the darkest pigment available at the time. What Haber achieved in the laboratory, Carl Bosch, the chief engineer of the German chemical giant BASF, refined into an industrial process capable of producing hundreds of tons of nitrogen in a factory the size of a small city, operated by more than fifty thousand workers. The Haber–Bosch process is the most important chemical discovery of the twentieth century. By doubling the amount of disposable nitrogen, it provoked the demographic explosion that took the human population from 1.6 to 7 billion in fewer than one hundred years. Today, nearly fifty per cent of the nitrogen atoms in our bodies are artificially created, and more than half the world population depends on foodstuffs fertilized thanks to Haber's invention. The modern world could not exist without "the man who pulled bread from air", in the words of the press of the day, though the immediate aim of his miraculous discovery was not to feed the hungry masses but to provide Germany with the raw materials required to continue manufacturing gunpowder and explosives during the First World War once the English fleet had blocked its access to Chilean nitrate. Haber's nitrogen allowed the European conflict to drag on for two more years, raising the casualties on each side by several millions.

One of those who suffered from the prolongation of the war was a young cadet of twenty-five; an aspiring artist, he had done everything in his power to avoid military service, until at last the police arrived at 34 Schleißheimer Straße in Munich in January 1914. Threatened with prison, he appeared for his medical check-up in Salzburg, where he was declared "unfit, too weak to bear arms". In August of that year—when thousands of men registered for the army voluntarily, unable to contain their enthusiasm to participate in the war to come—the young painter's attitude suddenly changed: he wrote a personal letter to King Ludwig III of Bavaria, petitioning him for the right to serve as an Austrian in the Bavarian army. His permission arrived the next day.

Adi, as he was affectionately known to his comrades in the List Regiment, was sent directly to the battle that would come to be known in Germany as the *Kindermord bei Ypern*— the massacre of the innocents at Ypres—for the forty thousand young enlistees who lost their lives in only twenty days. Of the two hundred and fifty men who made up his company, only forty would survive. Adi was one of them. He received the Iron Cross, was promoted to lance corporal and named message-runner for his regiment, so spent several years at a comfortable distance from the front, reading political texts and playing with a stray dog he adopted and named Fuchsl—little fox. He filled the dead hours of war by painting bluish watercolours and making charcoal sketches of his pet and of life in the barracks. On October 15, 1918, while he lay about waiting for new orders, he was briefly blinded in a mustard gas attack launched by the English, and spent the final weeks of the war convalescing in a hospital in the small town of Pasewalk, in the north of Pomerania, his eyes transformed into two red-hot coals. When he learned of Germany's defeat, and of the abdication signed by Kaiser Wilhelm II, he suffered a second attack of blindness, different from the one caused by the gas: "Everything went black before my eyes. I tottered and groped my way back to the dormitory, threw myself on my bunk, and dug my burning head into my blankets and pillow," he remembered years later, in a cell in Landsberg prison, accused of treason as leader of a failed putsch. He spent nine months there, consumed by hatred, humiliated by the conditions the victorious parties had imposed on his adopted country, and feeling betrayed by the cowardice of the generals, who had surrendered rather than fighting to the last man. He planned his vengeance from prison in a book that described his personal struggle and outlined a plan to raise Germany above all the nations of the world—something he was prepared to do with his own hands, should it prove necessary. In the interwar years, while Adi climbed to the summit of the National Socialist Workers' Party, shouting the racist and anti-Semitic harangues that would eventually see him crowned Führer of all Germany, Fritz Haber was making his own efforts to restore his homeland's tarnished glory.

Emboldened by his successes with nitrogen, Haber proposed to reconstitute the Weimar Republic and pay the war reparations that were strangling its economy through a process as wondrous as the one that had won him the Nobel Prize: harvesting gold from the waves of the sea. Travelling under a false identity to avoid raising suspicions, he gathered five thousand samples of water from assorted seas across the globe, including bits of ice from the North Pole and Antarctica. He was convinced he could mine the gold dissolved in the oceans, but after years of arduous labour had to accept that his original calculations had overestimated the quantities of this precious metal by several orders of magnitude. He returned to his country empty-handed.

In Germany, he found refuge in his work as director of the Kaiser Wilhelm Institute for Physical Chemistry and Electrochemistry as anti-Semitism continued to flourish around him. Protected, for the moment, in his academic oasis, Haber and his team produced a number of new substances: one of them used cyanide in a pesticidal fumigant so destructive it was dubbed *Zyklon*, the German word for *cyclone*. The compound's extraordinary effectiveness stunned the entomologists who used it for the first time to delouse a ship covering the Hamburg–New York route. They wrote directly to Haber to praise "the extreme elegance of the eradication process". This new success led to Haber's promotion to National Commissioner for Pest Control, from which post he organized the extermination of bedbugs and fleas on the navy's submarines, and of rats and cockroaches in the army barracks. He fought against a veritable legion of moths that attacked the flour the government stored in a network of silos that stretched from Flensburg to Freiburg, which Haber described to his superiors as "a biblical plague that threatens the well-being of the German *Lebensraum*", unaware that they had already begun the persecution of all those who shared his Jewish roots.

Haber had converted to Christianity at twenty-five years old. He identified so closely with his country and its customs that his sons knew nothing of their ancestry until he told them they would have to flee Germany. Haber escaped after them and sought asylum in England, but his British colleagues scorned him, aware of his instrumental role in chemical warfare. He had to leave the island not long after arriving. Thenceforth, he would travel from country to country in the hope of reaching Palestine, his chest gripped with pain, his arteries incapable of delivering sufficient blood to his heart. He died in Basle in 1934, clutching the canister of nitroglycerine he needed to dilate his coronary vessels, not knowing that, years later, the Nazis would use in their gas chambers the pesticide he had helped create to murder his half-sister, his brother-in-law, his nephews and countless other Jews who died hunkered down, muscles cramping, skin covered with red and green spots, bleeding from their ears, spitting foam from their mouths, the young ones crushing the children and the elderly as they attempted to scale the heap of naked bodies and breathe a few more minutes, a few more seconds, because Zyklon B tended to pool on the floor after being dropped through hatches in the roof. When ventilators had diffused the cloud of cyanide, the bodies were dragged to enormous ovens and incinerated. The ashes were buried in pit graves, dumped in rivers and ponds, or scattered as fertilizer in the surrounding fields.

Among the few possessions Fritz Haber had with him when he died was a letter written to his wife. In it, he confessed that he felt an unbearable guilt; not for the part he had played, directly or indirectly, in the death of untold human beings, but because his method of extracting nitrogen from the air had so altered the natural equilibrium of the planet that he feared the world's future belonged not to mankind but to plants, as all that was needed was a drop in population to pre-modern levels for just a few decades to allow them to grow without limit, taking advantage of the excess nutrients humanity had bestowed upon them to spread out across the earth and cover it completely, suffocating all forms of life beneath a terrible verdure.

Schwarzschild's Singularity

On December 24, 1915, while drinking tea in his apartment in Berlin, Albert Einstein received an envelope sent from the trenches of the First World War.

The envelope had crossed a continent in flames; it was wrinkled, grubby and covered in mud, one corner was completely torn off, and the sender's name was obscured by a large bloodstain. Einstein handled it with gloves and slit it open with a knife. Inside he found a letter bearing the last spark of a true genius: Karl Schwarzschild, astronomer, physicist, mathematician and lieutenant in the German army.

"As you see, the war treated me kindly enough, in spite of the heavy gunfire, to allow me to get away from it all and take this walk in the land of your ideas" were the final words of the letter Einstein read completely dumbfounded—not because one of the most respected scientists in Germany was commanding an artillery unit on the Russian front, nor because of his friend's cryptic warnings about a coming catastrophe, but due to what was written on the back of the page: in a minuscule hand that Einstein could only decipher with a magnifying glass, Schwarzschild had sent him the first exact solution to the equations of general relativity.

Einstein had to reread it several times. When had he published his theory? A month ago? Less than a month? It was impossible for Schwarzschild to have solved such complex equations in so little time, if even he—who had created them!—had only been capable of finding approximate solutions. Schwarzschild's solution was precise: it perfectly described the manner in which the mass of a star deforms the space and time surrounding it.

Although he was holding the solution in his hands, Einstein could scarcely believe it. He knew these results would be fundamental to generating greater interest in his theory among the scientific community, which until then had viewed it with little enthusiasm, largely because of its complexity. He had already resigned himself to the possibility that no one would find a precise solution to his equations— at least not during his lifetime. That Schwarzschild had done so among mortar explosions and clouds of poison gas was a proper miracle. "I had not expected that one could formulate the exact solution of the problem in such a simple way!" he responded to Schwarzschild as soon as he had composed himself and promised to present his work to the Academy, unaware that he was writing to a dead man.

The trick Schwarzschild had used was simple: he analysed an ideal, perfectly spherical star, without rotation or electric charge, then employed Einstein's equations to calculate how that mass would alter the form of space, analogous to the way a cannonball placed on a bed would deform the mattress.

His measurements were so precise that even today they are used to trace out the paths of the stars, the orbits of planets and the distortions undergone by rays of light as they pass near a body that exerts a significant gravitational pull.

Yet there was something deeply strange about Schwarzs-child's results.

They worked flawlessly for an ordinary star, around which space curved softly, just as Einstein predicted, and the body of the star remained suspended in the centre of a depression, like a pair of children resting inside a cloth hammock. The problem arose when too much mass was concentrated in a very small area, as occurs when a giant star exhausts its fuel and begins to collapse. According to Schwarzschild's calculations, in such a case, space-time would not simply bend; it would tear apart. The star would go on compressing and its density would increase till the force of gravity became so powerful that space would become infinitely curved, closing in on itself. The result would be an inescapable abyss permanently cut off from the rest of the universe.

They called this the *Schwarzschild singularity.*

Initially, even Schwarzschild cast this result aside as a mathematical anomaly. After all, physics is rife with infinities that are nothing more than numbers on paper, abstractions that do not represent real-world objects, or that simply indicate calculating errors. The singularity in his metrics was undoubtedly one of these: a mistake, an oddity, a metaphysical delirium.

Because the alternative was unthinkable. At a certain distance from Schwarzschild's idealized star, the equations of general relativity went mad: time froze, space coiled around itself like a serpent. At the centre of that dying star, all mass became concentrated in a single point of infinite density. For Schwarzschild, that such a thing could exist in the universe was inconceivable. Not only did it defy common sense and cast doubts on general relativity, it threatened the very foundations of physics, as, within the singularity, the notions of space and time themselves became meaningless. Schwarzschild attempted to find a logical solution to the paradox he had created. Did the fault lie in his conceit? Had he simply been too clever for his own good? Because in the real world, there was no such thing as a perfectly spherical, completely immobile star, with no electric charge. Surely the anomaly arose from the ideal conditions he had tried to impose on the world, impossible to replicate in reality. His singularity, he told himself, was nothing but an imaginary monster. A paper tiger, a Chinese dragon.

And yet, he could not get it out of his head. Even immersed in the chaos of war, the singularity spread across his mind like a stain, superimposed over the hellscape of the trenches; he saw it in the eyes of the dead horses buried in the muck, in the bullet wounds of his fellow soldiers, in the shadowy lenses of their hideous gas masks. His imagination had fallen prey to the pull of his discovery: with alarm, he realized that if his singularity were ever to exist, it would endure until the end of the universe. Its ideal conditions made it an eternal object that would neither grow nor diminish, but remain eternally as it was. Unlike all other things, it was immune to becoming and doubly inescapable: in the strange spatial geometry it generated, the singularity was located at both ends of time: one could flee from it into the remotest past or escape to the furthest future only to encounter it once more. In the last letter he sent to his wife from Russia, written the same day he chose to share his discovery with Einstein, Schwarzschild complains of something strange that has begun to grow inside him: "I don't know how to name or define it, but it has an irrepressible force and darkens all my thoughts. It is a void without form or dimension, a shadow I can't see, but one that I can feel with the entirety of my soul."

Soon afterwards, that shadow invaded his body.

His sickness began with two blisters at the corner of his mouth. Within a month, they covered his hands, feet, throat, lips, neck and genitals. After two, he was dead.

The military physicians diagnosed him with pemphigus, a disease in which the body fails to recognize its own cells and attacks them violently. Ashkenazi Jews show a particular susceptibility. The doctors who treated him told him it might have been triggered by a gas attack that had taken place months before, one that Schwarzschild described in his diaries: "The moon crossed the sky so quickly, it seemed time itself had sped up. My soldiers readied their arms and waited for the order to attack, but the phenomenon was so strange and unsettling, they thought it a bad omen, and I could see the fear in their eyes." Schwarzschild tried to explain to them that the nature of the moon had not changed; it was an optical illusion, caused by a thin layer of clouds crossing in front of it, making it seem larger and faster than it was. He spoke to them with the same tenderness he would have used with his children, but he did not manage to convince them. Nor could he himself shake off the feeling that everything had begun to move more swiftly since the start of the war, as though the world was slipping off a precipice. When the clouds cleared, he saw two horsemen at full gallop, followed by a dense mist that advanced towards them like the waves of the sea. The fog spread across the whole of the horizon, as solid as the sheer walls of a cliff, and from a distance it appeared immobile, but soon it had enveloped the hooves of the horses, and the animals and their riders tumbled to the ground. Alarm echoed throughout the trenches and Schwarzschild managed to help two soldiers who were petrified with fear to adjust the rubber straps on their masks, but he had hardly managed to don his own before the cloud of gas settled over them.

At the start of the war, Schwarzschild was more than forty years old, and director of the most prestigious observatory in Germany. Either of those would have sufficed to exempt him from active service. But Schwarzschild was a man of honour who loved his country, and, like thousands of other Jews, he was anxious to show his patriotism. He enlisted voluntarily, deaf to the counsel of his friends and the warnings of his wife.

Before witnessing the cruel reality of combat and suffering the horror of modern war in his own flesh, Schwarzschild had found the camaraderie of the army rejuvenating. When his unit was first deployed, he discovered a system for perfecting the sights on the tanks—without anyone having requested that he do so—tinkering with them in his free time with the same eagerness with which he had built his first telescope, as if the drills and simulations of his months of training had rekindled in him the boundless curiosity he had known during childhood.

He had grown up obsessed by light. At seven, he took apart his father's glasses and placed the lenses inside a rolled-up newspaper to show his brother the rings of Saturn. He passed entire nights without sleep, peering up at the sky, even when it was completely cloudy. His father, unnerved to see his son spellbound by that darkened firmament, asked him what he was searching for. The boy told him there was a star hiding behind the clouds that he alone could see.

From the time he learnt to talk, he spoke of nothing but celestial bodies. He was the first scientist in a family of merchants and artists. At sixteen, he published a paper in the prestigious journal *Astronomische Nachrichten* about the orbits of binary stars. Before he had turned twenty, he had written about the evolution of stars, from their formation as clouds of gas to their catastrophic final explosion—and had invented a system of his own for measuring the intensity of their light.

He was convinced that mathematics, physics and astronomy constituted a single body of knowledge and believed that Germany was capable of exercising a civilizing force comparable to that of ancient Greece. To do so, however, its science must be raised to the heights already achieved by its philosophy and art, for "only a vision of the whole, like that of a saint, a madman or a mystic, will permit us to decipher the true organizing principles of the universe."

As a child, he had close-set eyes, big ears, a button nose, thin lips and a pointy chin; as an adult, a broad forehead, sparse hair hinting at an eventual baldness that did not have time to develop, an intelligent gaze and a roguish smile hidden behind an imperial moustache as thick as Nietzsche's.

He attended a Jewish primary school, where he tried the patience of the rabbis with questions to which they lacked answers: what was the true significance of that passage in the Book of Job which says that Yahweh *stretcheth out the north over the empty place, and hangeth the earth upon nothing?* In the margins of his notebooks, next to the arithmetic problems that so frustrated his classmates, Schwarzschild calculated the equilibrium of liquid bodies in rotation, desperately trying to prove the long-term stability of the rings of Saturn, which he saw coming apart over and over in a recurring nightmare. To lighten his obsessions, his father obliged him to take piano lessons. At the end of his second lesson, young Schwarzschild opened the lid of the instrument and unwound its strings to understand the underlying logic of its tones; he had read Johannes Kepler's *Harmonice Mundi*, which expressed the view that each planet generated a melody in its transit around the sun, a music of the spheres that our ears were incapable of distinguishing but that the human mind was able to decipher.

He never lost the capacity for astonishment: when he was a student at university, he observed a total eclipse from the heights of the Jungfraujoch, and though he understood the mechanism responsible for the phenomenon, he struggled to believe that a mass as small as the moon could blanket all of Europe in the deepest darkness. "How strange space is, and how capricious the laws of optics and perspective, that they should permit even the smallest child to cover the sun with one of his fingers," he wrote to his brother Alfred, a painter who lived in Hamburg.

For his doctoral thesis, he calculated the deformation undergone by satellites subject to the gravitational pull of the planets they orbit. The mass of the earth, for example, generates a tide that crosses the surface of the moon, just as the moon itself gives rise to a tide in our oceans. In the former case, this is a wave of solid rock four metres high propagated over the moon's crust. The attraction between the two bodies synchronizes their rotation periods perfectly: as the moon turns on its axis at the same speed as it rotates around our planet, one of its faces is eternally hidden from view. This dark side remained beyond the reach of our knowledge from the birth of the human race until 1959, when the Soviet probe Luna 3 photographed it for the first time.

During his internship at the Kuffner observatory, one of the binary stars of the Auriga constellation, just off the shoulder of Orion, went nova. For several days, it was the brightest object in the sky. The white dwarf in this dyad, which had remained dormant for aeons after having exhausted its fuel, began to draw on the gases of its red giant companion star and returned to life with a colossal explosion. Schwarzschild spent three days and nights awake, observing it; to understand the catastrophic death of stars seemed to him essential for the future survival of our species; if one of them exploded near the earth, it would burn up our atmosphere and extinguish all forms of life.

The day after he turned twenty-eight, he became the youngest university professor in Germany. He was appointed director of the observatory at the University of Göttingen, despite his refusal to undergo the Christian baptism required to take the position.

In 1905, he travelled to Algeria to observe a total eclipse, but he failed to heed the maximum exposure time and damaged the cornea of his left eye. When they removed the patch he had been forced to wear for weeks, he noticed a shadow the size of a two-mark coin in his visual field, which was apparent even when his eyes were closed. The doctors told him the damage was irreversible. To his friends, who worried about the effects eventual blindness might have on an astronomer's career, he said—only partly in jest—that he, like Odin, had sacrificed one eye to be able to see further with the other.

As though to prove that the accident had in no way diminished his faculties, that year Schwarzschild worked like a man possessed, publishing article after article. He analysed the transport of energy through stars by means of radiation, carried out studies of the equilibrium in the atmosphere of the sun, described the distribution of astral velocities and proposed a mechanism for modelling radiative transfer. Arthur Eddington compared him to a guerrilla leader, as "his attacks fell where they were least expected and his joy was to range unrestricted over the pastures of knowledge." Alarmed by the manic fervour of his academic output, his colleagues advised him to slow down, fearing that his inner fire would consume him. Schwarzschild paid them no attention. Physics was not enough for him. He aspired to the type of knowledge the alchemists had pursued, and laboured beneath the sway of a strange urgency that not even he could fully explain: "Often I have been unfaithful to the heavens. My interest has never been limited to things situated in space, beyond the moon, but has rather followed those threads woven between them and the darkest zones of the human soul, as it is there that the new light of science must be shone."

In all that he did, Schwarzschild would take things to the limit; during an expedition to the Alps, at the invitation of his brother Alfred, he ordered their guides to loosen the ropes at the most dangerous part of a glacier crossing, putting the entire expedition at risk, merely so that he could get closer to two of his colleagues and solve a problem that they had been working on together, by scraping equations into the permafrost with their pickaxes. His recklessness so angered his brother that the two of them never climbed together again, although they had spent nearly every weekend in their university days exploring the mountains of the Black Forest. Alfred was aware of the extent of his brother's obsessiveness: the year of his graduation, a snowstorm had stranded them on one of the ledges of the Brocken, the highest peak of the Harz mountain range. To keep from freezing to death, they had had to build a shelter and sleep holding one another, as they had when they were children. They survived on a bag of walnuts, but when they ran out of water and matches to melt the snow, they had to brave the descent in the middle of the night, their way brightened solely by the light of the stars. Alfred was terrified and kept tripping, though he arrived unharmed. His brother Karl did not misstep a single time, as if he were somehow capable of seeing the trail in the dark, but was left with nerve damage in his right hand from the cold; in the shelter, he had repeatedly removed his gloves to revise his calculations concerning a series of elliptical curves.

When he conducted experiments he was no less impulsive: he would remove pieces from one instrument to use them for another, without leaving any record of what he had done. If he needed a diaphragm in a hurry, he would simply drill a hole in the lens cap. When he left Göttingen to oversee the observatory in Potsdam, his replacement nearly quit before his appointment had begun: upon taking an inventory, in order to determine how badly the facilities had suffered under Schwarzschild, he found a transparency of the Venus di Milo inside the focal plane of the largest telescope, arranged in such a way that the stars of the Cassiopeia constellation outlined the goddess's arms.

He was extraordinarily awkward around women. Although his female students pursued him, and referred to him as "the professor with the shining eyes", he did not dare to kiss his future wife, Else Rosenbach, until the second time he had asked her to marry him. Else had rejected his first proposal out of fear that his interest in her was purely intellectual; Schwarzschild was so timid that he had only touched her once during their long courtship, and, even then, it had been by mistake: he had laid a hand on her breast while helping her focus on the star Polaris through the lens of a small, homemade telescope. They married in 1909, had a daughter, Agatha, and two sons, Martin and Alfred. The girl studied classics and became an expert in Greek philology; the older brother became a professor of astrophysics at Princeton, while the younger, born with an irregular heartbeat and perpetually dilated pupils, suffered multiple nervous breakdowns throughout his life, and committed suicide on finding himself unable to escape from Germany after the persecution of the Jews began.

Like many sensitive people, Schwarzschild felt overcome by a sense of imminent disaster as the First World War approached. In him, this took the peculiar form of a fear that physics would be incapable of explaining the movement of the stars, or of finding an order in the universe. "Is there anything that is truly at rest, something stationary around which the universe revolves, or is there nothing at all to hold on to amid this endless chain of movements in which every single thing seems bound? Just imagine how far we have fallen into uncertainty if the human imagination cannot find a single place to lay its anchor, if not a single stone in the world has the right to be considered immobile!" Schwarzschild dreamt of the coming of a new Copernicus, someone who could model the intricacies of celestial mechanics and reveal the pattern dictating the complex orbits the stars trace out in the firmament. The alternative was unbearable: that there was nothing more than lifeless spheres in the throes of random chance, "like the molecules of a gas that float from one place to the other in a completely irregular manner, so much so that their very chaos is being enthroned as principle." In Potsdam, he created an enormous network of colleagues to follow and register, with the maximum possible precision, the movements of more than two million stars. His hope was not only to understand the logic of their orbits, but to decipher where they would lead us. Because while the movement of two bodies bound by gravitation can be known with precision according to the laws of Newton, the addition of a third renders it unforeseeable. Schwarzschild believed that our own planetary system was completely unstable in the long term. Its present order might be vouchsafed for a million or even a billion years, but, with time, the planets would escape from their orbits, the gaseous giants would engulf their neighbours, and Earth itself would be expelled from the solar system to roam, like a wandering star, until the end of time, unless the form of space were not planar. Anticipating Einstein, Schwarzschild had considered the hypothesis that the geometry of the universe was less like a three-dimensional box than something that could be twisted and deformed. In his article "On the Admissible Curvature of Space" he analysed the possibility that we inhabited a semi-spherical universe, yielding a world that would turn in on itself like an ouroboros: "We would be faced with a fairyland geometry, a hall of mirrors whose horrifying perspectives would be more than the civilized mind could bear, as it abhors and flees from all it cannot comprehend." In 1910, he discovered that the stars had different colours, and he was the first to analyse them, using a special camera he had built with the assistance of the Potsdam observatory's porter—the only other Jew who worked there, with whom he often drank till dawn. Attaching this camera to the porter's broom and swinging it in circles, he took photographs from a number of angles to confirm the existence of red giants, monstrous stars hundreds of times larger than our sun. His favourite—Antares—was the colour of a ruby. The Arabs called it *Kalb al-Akrab*, the heart of the scorpion; the Greeks considered it the only rival of Ares. In April, Schwarzschild organized a journey to Tenerife to photograph the return of Halley's Comet, which had always been considered an ill omen: in the year 66, the historian Flavius Josephus had described it as "a star that resembles a sword", come to warn of the destruction of Jerusalem by the Romans, while in 1222 its appearance in the sky had inspired Genghis Khan to invade Europe. It struck Schwarzschild as fascinating that the long wake of its tail—which the earth crossed, on this occasion, over the course of six hours—always lay in the direction opposite to that of the sun. "What wind drags it off with the fury of an angel cast out from Heaven, falling and falling and falling?"

When war broke out four years later, Schwarzschild was among the first to volunteer.

He was assigned to the battalion that laid siege to Namur, in Belgium, to reinforce the German bombardment, trying to break the ring of fortresses surrounding the thousand-year-old city. As Schwarzschild had trained at a meteorological station, he was posted to lead the charge. The Germans' advance was impeded by a mist that rose up without warning, so thick it turned midday to night. Both sides were shrouded in darkness and unable to attack for fear of shooting their own men. "What is it about the strange, chaotic climate of this country that it so doggedly resists our knowledge and control?" he wrote to his wife after a week of work to counteract the effects of the mist or, at least, predict the moment when it might occur. When he failed to do so, his superior chose to withdraw the troops to a safe distance and engaged in massive, indiscriminate bombings, firing without care for wasted munitions or civilian casualties, using 42-centimetre ordnance shot from a gigantic howitzer the troops nicknamed "Big Bertha", until the citadel, which had stood fast from the time of the Roman Empire, was nothing more than a mountain of rubble.

From there, Schwarzschild was transferred to the 5th Army artillery regiment, entrenched in the forest of Argonne on the French front. When he presented himself to the officers in charge, they ordered him to calculate the trajectories of twenty-five thousand shells loaded with mustard gas, which would fall on the French troops in the middle of the night. "They ask me to predict the winds and storms, when we ourselves are the ones stoking the fires that rage behind them. They want to know the ideal trajectory that will lead our projectiles to the enemy, and don't see the ellipse that will drag all of us down. I am tired of hearing the officers say that we are ever closer to victory, and that the end of the war is in reach. Don't they understand that we are rising up only to fall?"

Not even in the midst of the butchery of war did he abandon his research. He carried his notebook beneath his uniform, close to his chest. When he was promoted to lieutenant, he took advantage of his newfound privileges to ask that the most recent publications in physics be sent to him from Germany. In November 1915, he read the equations of general relativity published in *Annalen der Physik* no. 39 and began working out the solution he would send Einstein one month later. From that moment onwards, he underwent a change that would even affect his manner of note-taking. His handwriting became smaller, to the point of becoming practically illegible. In his diary, and in the letters he sent to his wife, his patriotic zeal gives way to bitter complaints about the meaninglessness of the war and a growing contempt for the stupidity of his fellow officers that would only increase as his calculations came closer to the singularity. When he finally reached it, he could think of nothing more: he became so immersed that he failed to take cover during an enemy attack, and a mortar exploded a few metres away from his head. No one understood how he had survived.

Before winter came, they shipped him off to the eastern front. The soldiers he came across shared rumours of horrible massacres of civilians, lootings, rapes and deportations. Whole towns decimated in the course of a single night. Cities with no strategic value that vanished from the map as though they had never existed. The atrocities committed obeyed no martial logic; often it was impossible to know which of the two sides was responsible. When Schwarzschild saw a group of his soldiers practising their aim on a scrawny dog quivering some way away, panicked and incapable of fleeing, something broke inside him. The drawings he was used to making of the daily life of his comrades or the splendours of the countryside—which grew colder and more forbidding the further they advanced—gave way to whole pages covered in thick lines of charcoal and black spirals that vanished past the edges of the page. At the end of November, his battalion joined the 10th Army on the outskirts of Kosava, in Belarus. From there, he sent a letter to Ejnar Hertzsprung, a colleague from the University of Potsdam, which included a draft of his singularity, a description of the blisters that had begun to appear on his skin, and a long digression on the insidious effects the war might have on Germany's soul, a country Schwarzschild continued to love, but that he saw reeling on the edge of an abyss: "We have reached the highest point of civilization. All that is left for us is to decay and fall."

Pemphigus, acute necrotizing ulcerative gingivitis. The blisters in his oesophagus prevented him from swallowing solid food. Those in his mouth and throat burned like hot coals whenever he tried to drink water. Schwarzschild was given a furlough by the doctors, but he continued to work on the equations of general relativity, unable to control the manic speeding of his mind, which accelerated as the illness consumed the rest of his body. He published 112 articles in total during his lifetime, more than virtually any other scientist in the twentieth century. The final ones he composed on sheets of paper laid out on the floor, his arms hanging over the edge of his bed, lying on his stomach, covered in scabs and abscesses left behind by his blisters when they burst, his body transformed, as it were, into a miniature model of war-torn Europe. To distract himself from the pain, he catalogued the shape and distribution of his wounds, the surface tension of the fluid building up in his blisters, and the average time they required to rupture, but still he could not tear his mind from the void his equations had opened up.

He filled three notebooks with calculations meant to explain away the singularity, in the hope of finding a pathway out or an error in his reasoning. In the last of these, Schwarzschild deduced that any object could generate a singularity if its matter were compressed into a sufficiently restricted space: for the sun, three kilometres, for the earth, eight millimetres, and 0.00000000000000000000001 centimetres for the mass of an average human body.

Inside the void his metrics predicted, the fundamental parameters of the universe switched properties: space flowed like time, time stretched out like space. This distortion altered the law of causality; Schwarzschild deduced that if a hypothetical traveller were capable of surviving a journey through this rarefied zone, he would receive light and information from the future, which would allow him to see events that had not yet occurred. If he could reach the centre of the abyss without gravity tearing him apart, he would distinguish two superimposed images projected at once in a small circle over his head, like those that are visible through a kaleidoscope: in one, he would perceive the entire future evolution of the universe at an inconceivable pace, in the other, the past frozen in a single instant.

The anomalies were not confined to the singularity's interior. Around it, there existed a limit, a barrier that marked a point of no return. After crossing that line, any object—from a whole planet to a minuscule subatomic particle—would be trapped forever. It would disappear from the universe as though it had fallen into a bottomless pit.

Decades later, this limit was dubbed *the Schwarzschild radius.*

Einstein wrote a eulogy for him after his death, and read it aloud during his funeral. "He fought against the problems from which others fled. He loved discovering the relations between multiple aspects of nature, but what drove his search was joy, the pleasure an artist feels, the vertigo of the visionary capable of discerning the threads that weave the fabric of the future," he said to the small group of men gathered before his tomb. None of them suspected how much Schwarzschild had been tormented by his greatest discovery, as not even Einstein himself could understand what takes place when equations bleed into the singular and infinity appears as their only possible result.

The young mathematician Richard Courant was the last person to speak directly to Schwarzschild, and the only one who could attest to the effects the singularity wrought on the astrophysicist's mind.

Courant had been wounded in Rava-Ruska; he met Schwarzschild in the military hospital. The young man had been assistant to David Hilbert, one of the most influential German mathematicians of his era, so he recognized Schwarzschild right away, despite the wounds that disfigured his face. He approached him timidly, not comprehending how a man of his prestige and intellectual standing had been sent to so dangerous a place. In his diary, Courant described how the eyes of Lieutenant Schwarzschild, darkened by battle, lit up as soon as he heard the ideas Hilbert was developing. The two men spoke throughout the night. Close to dawn, Schwarzschild spoke to him of the rupture he believed he had discovered.

According to Schwarzschild, the most frightful thing about mass at its most extreme degree of concentration was not the way it altered the form of space, or the strange effects it exerted on time: the true horror, he said, was that the singularity was a blind spot, fundamentally unknowable. Light could never escape from it, so our eyes were incapable of seeing it. Nor could our minds grasp it, because at the singularity the laws of general relativity simply broke down. Physics no longer had any meaning.

Courant listened to him, rapt. Just before the doctors came looking for him and the young man rejoined the convoy that would take him back to Berlin, Schwarzschild asked him a question that tormented him for the rest of his life, though at the time he considered it nothing but the ravings of a dying soldier, product of a creeping madness that had overtaken Schwarzschild's mind as weariness and despair consumed him.

If matter were prone to birthing monsters of this kind, Schwarzschild asked with a trembling voice, were there correlations with the human psyche? Could a sufficient concentration of human will—millions of people exploited for a single end with their minds compressed into the same psychic space—unleash something comparable to the singularity? Schwarzschild was convinced that such a thing was not only possible, but was actually taking place in the Fatherland. Courant tried to appease him; he said that he saw no signs of the apocalypse Schwarzschild feared, and that surely there could be nothing worse than the war they were mired in. He reminded Schwarzschild that the human soul was a greater mystery than any mathematical enigma, and that it was unwise to project the findings of physics into such far-flung realms as psychology. But Schwarzschild was inconsolable. He babbled about a black sun dawning over the horizon, capable of engulfing the entire world, and he lamented that there was nothing we could do about it. Because the singularity sent forth no warnings. The point of no return—the limit past which one fell prey to its unforgiving pull—had no sign or demarcation. Whoever crossed it was beyond hope. Their destiny was set, as all possible trajectories led irrevocably to the singularity. And if such was the nature of that threshold, Schwarzschild asked, his eyes shot through with blood, how would we know if we had already crossed it?

Courant left to return to Germany. Schwarzschild died that afternoon.

*   *   *

More than two decades would pass before the scientific community would accept Schwarzschild's ideas as an inevitable consequence of the theory of relativity.

Einstein himself was the one who fought hardest to exorcise the demon Schwarzschild had invoked. In 1939, he published his article "On a Stationary System with Spherical Symmetry Consisting of Many Gravitational Masses", which explained why singularities such as those Schwarzschild described could not exist. "The singularity does not appear for the simple reason that matter cannot be concentrated arbitrarily. And this is due to the fact that otherwise the constituting particles would reach the speed of light." With characteristic intelligence, the German-born physicist had appealed to the internal logic of his theory to patch the rent in the fabric of space-time, protecting the universe from a catastrophic gravitational collapse.

But the calculations of the greatest mind of the twentieth century were wrong.

On September 1, 1939—the same day the Nazi tanks crossed the Polish frontier—Robert Oppenheimer and Hartland Snyder published an article in Volume 56 of the *Physical Review*. In it, the two physicists from North America demonstrated beyond all shadow of a doubt that "When all thermonuclear sources of energy are exhausted a sufficiently heavy star will collapse. Unless it reduces its mass due to fission, rotation or radiation, this contraction will continue indefinitely," forming the black hole that Schwarzschild had prophesied, *capable of crumpling space like a piece of paper and extinguishing time like a blown-out candle*, and no natural law or physical force could avert it.

The Heart of
the Heart

On the morning of August 31, 2012, the Japanese mathematician Shinichi Mochizuki published four articles on his blog. Those six hundred pages contained a proof of one of the most important conjectures in number theory, known as $a + b = c$.

To this day, no one has managed to comprehend it.

Mochizuki had worked for years in complete isolation, developing a mathematical theory that bore no resemblance to any that had been known before.

He gave his discovery no publicity after uploading it to his blog, neither sending it to specialized publications nor presenting it at conferences. One of the first people to become aware of its existence was Akio Tamagawa, his colleague at the Research Institute for Mathematical Sciences at the University of Kyoto, who sent the articles to Ivan Fesenko, a number theorist at the University of Nottingham, attached to an email with a single question:

"Has Mochizuki solved $a + b = c$?"

Fesenko could hardly contain his impatience as he saved the four huge files to his computer. He spent ten minutes watching the download bar, and then shut himself away for two weeks to study the proof, ordering takeaway meals and sleeping only when exhaustion demanded it. He responded to Tamagawa with three words:

"Impossible to understand."

In December 2013, a year after Mochizuki published his articles, several of the most prominent mathematicians in the world gathered in Oxford to study the proof. Enthusiasm reigned during the early days of the seminar. The obscure reasoning of the Japanese mathematician had begun to yield to comprehension, and, on the third night, the rumour that a major step forward was about to take place spread on internet forums and specialized websites.

On the fourth day, everything collapsed.

After a certain point, no one was capable of following the proof's arguments any further. The greatest mathematical minds on the planet were baffled, and there was nobody who could help them, since Mochizuki himself had refused to participate in the meeting.

The new branch of mathematics that Shinichi Mochizuki had created to prove the conjecture was so bizarre, abstract and ahead of its time that a theoretician from the University of Wisconsin–Madison said that he felt as though he was studying a paper from the future: "Everybody who I'm aware of who's come close to this stuff is quite reasonable, but afterwards they become incapable of communicating it."

The few who have been able to follow Mochizuki's system sufficiently to understand it in part say it consists of a series of underlying relationships between numbers that are invisible at first sight. "If researchers want to apprehend my work, they must first deactivate the thought patterns that they have installed in their brains and taken for granted for so many years," Mochizuki wrote on his blog.

He was born in Tokyo, and from a young age was famous for his powers of concentration, which his peers have described as beyond human. As a child, he suffered attacks of muteness that became increasingly intense during his adolescence, to such an extent that hearing him talk became a rarity. Nor could he stand other people's gazes, and would walk with his eyes pinned to the ground, a habit which gave his back a slight hump that did not, however, diminish his good looks, as his high forehead, enormous glasses and dark, slicked-back hair gave him an uncanny resemblance to Superman's alter ego, Clark Kent.

He was sixteen when he entered Princeton, and by twenty-three he already had his doctorate. After spending two years at Harvard, he moved back to Japan, accepting a post as professor at the Research Institute for Mathematical Sciences at the University of Kyoto on condition that he be permitted to devote himself exclusively to research, with no obligation to teach classes. At the beginning of the 2000s, he stopped attending international conferences. Over the following years, his life became increasingly constricted. First he limited himself to travelling within Japan, then he no longer ventured beyond the Kyoto prefecture, and finally his range was confined to the narrow circuit between his apartment and his tiny office at the university.

From the window of that office, as orderly as the interior of a temple, there is a view of Mount Daimonji, where once a year, during the O-Bon festival, the monks burn a giant kanji in the form of a man with outstretched arms – 大 – a sign which means enormous/tall/monumental, and is used to express extreme grandiloquence, similar to that employed by Mochizuki in christening his new branch of mathematics, which he called, without a trace of either modesty or irony, Inter-Universal Teichmüller Theory.

The $a + b = c$ conjecture reaches down to the roots of mathematics. It proposes a deep and unexpected relationship between the additive and multiplicative properties of numbers. If it is proven, it will become a formidable tool capable of dispelling, as if by magic, a vast quantity of long-standing enigmas. But Mochizuki's ambition was even greater than that; he did not stop at verifying the conjecture, but even invented a novel type of geometry, one that required mathematicians to conceive of numbers in a radically different way. According to Yuichiro Yamashita, one of the few who claims to have grasped the real scope of his Inter-Universal Theory, Mochizuki has created a complete universe, of which, for the moment, he is the sole inhabitant.

But extraordinary claims require extraordinary evidence, and Mochizuki's refusal to give interviews, defend his results in person, or even discuss his work in a language other than Japanese, made his peers suspicious. To some it was all an elaborate hoax, while others said that he suffered from an acute psychological imbalance, and offered as proof his growing social phobia and the isolation he worked in.

Things seemed to improve in 2014, when he announced that he would travel to France in November to present his theory during a six-day seminar at the University of Montpellier. Mathematicians from all over the world fought for a seat and even lined the stairs on both sides of the lecture room, but Mochizuki stood them all up. He had arrived a week in advance, suffered the overbearing attentions of the rector of the university, and then disappeared. No one knew where he was till the day before his talks were slated to begin, when the guards ejected him from the campus after a confusing incident.

As soon as he returned to Japan, Mochizuki removed the proof from his blog and threatened legal action against anyone who tried to publish it. He was subject to a wave of attacks from his most hardened critics, while his colleagues assumed that he had discovered a fundamental flaw in the logic of his proof. Mochizuki denied this, but offered no explanations. He renounced his post at the University of Kyoto, and wrote a last entry before shutting down his blog, stating that, in mathematics, certain things should remain hidden, "for the good of all of us". This incomprehensible and apparently capricious gesture only confirmed what many had feared: Mochizuki had succumbed to Grothendieck's curse.

Alexander Grothendieck was one of the most important mathematicians of the twentieth century. During a creative outburst almost unparalleled in the history of science, he revolutionized our understanding of space and time, not just once, but twice. Mochizuki's own fame dated from 1996, when he managed to prove one of Grothendieck's conjectures, and everyone who met the Japanese mathematician while he was still a student knew that he regarded Grothendieck as his master.

Required reading for mathematicians all over the world, Grothendieck had led a team that had produced tens of thousands of pages, a colossal, intimidating oeuvre into

which most undergraduates only dipped their toes to learn
what was necessary to advance in their own fields, but even
that could take years. Mochizuki, on the other hand, began
reading the first volume of Grothendieck's collected works
as a freshman and did not stop until he had finished the
last.

Minhyong Kim, Mochizuki's roommate at Princeton,
remembers having found him delirious at midnight after
days without sleep or food. Exhausted and dehydrated, he
babbled incoherently, his pupils as wide as an owl's. He spoke
of the "heart of the heart", an entity Grothendieck had
discovered at the very centre of mathematics, which had
completely unhinged him. The next morning, when Kim
asked for an explanation, Mochizuki stood and stared at
him. He had no memory of the night before.

*   *   *

Between 1958 and 1973, Alexander Grothendieck towered
over mathematics like a veritable colossus, convincing the
finest minds of his generation to put aside their own research
projects and ambitions and join his radical quest to unearth
the structures underlying all mathematical objects.

His method of working was extraordinary. Even though
he was able to solve three of the four Weil conjectures, the
greatest mathematical enigmas of his time, Grothendieck
was not interested in deciphering famous problems or
reaching seemingly unthinkable results; his desire was to
achieve an absolute understanding of the foundations of
mathematics. To do so, he constructed intricate theoretical
architectures around the simplest of questions, encircling
them with a vast array of new concepts. Under the soft,

continuous pressure of Grothendieck's reasoning, solutions seemed to reveal themselves of their own free will, welling up to the surface, and opening, as he once said, "like a nutshell that had spent months submerged in water".

His was the power of unbridled abstraction. He championed an approach that was based on wild generalizations, zooming further and further out and then focusing sharply, as any dilemma became clear when one viewed it from a sufficient distance. Numbers, angles, curves and equations did not interest him, nor did any other mathematical object in particular: all that he cared for was the relationship between them. "He had an extraordinary sensitivity to the harmony of things," one of his disciples, Luc Illusie, recalled. "Not only did he introduce new techniques and prove major theorems: he changed the way we think about mathematics."

Space was his lifelong obsession. One of his greatest strokes of genius was expanding the notion of the point. Beneath his gaze, the humble dot was no longer a dimensionless position; it swelled with a complex inner structure. Where others had seen a simple locus without depth, size or breadth, Grothendieck saw an entire universe. No one had proposed something so bold since Euclid.

For years, he devoted the whole of his energy, twelve hours a day, seven days a week, to mathematics. He did not read newspapers, watch television or go to the cinema. He liked ugly women, squalid apartments, dilapidated rooms. He worked cloistered in a cold office with flaking paint falling from the walls, his back turned to the only window, with pen and paper on his desk and only four objects as decoration: his mother's death mask, a small wire sculpture of a goat, a jar of Spanish olives, and a charcoal portrait of his father, drawn in Le Vernet concentration camp.

Alexander Schapiro, Alexander Tanaroff, Sascha, Piotr, Sergei. His father's real name has not come down to us, as he lived under multiple aliases while participating in the anarchist movements that rocked Europe at the beginning of the twentieth century. A Ukrainian from a Hasidic family, he was arrested by the Tsarist police at fifteen and sentenced to death along with his comrades. He was the only one to survive. For three weeks they dragged him from his cell to the execution ground, where he watched his friends die, one by one, before the firing squad. He was spared the death penalty on account of his age, condemned to life in prison, and freed ten years later, during the Russian Revolution of 1917. He dove head first into a series of conspiracies, secret plots and internal skirmishes between opposing revolutionary factions that cost him his left arm, though it remains unclear whether this was the result of combat, a frustrated assassination attempt, a failed suicide or a bomb that went off in his hand while he was still carrying it. He made his living as a street photographer. In Berlin, he met Grothendieck's mother, and the two of them moved to Paris in 1939. In 1940, he was arrested by the Vichy government and interned in Le Vernet. He was deported to Germany in 1942, and died of Zyklon B poisoning in one of the gas chambers at Auschwitz.

His son took the last name of his mother, Johanna Grothendieck, a woman who wrote her entire life, though she never managed to publish her novels or poems. When she met Grothendieck's father, she was married and working as a journalist for a leftist daily. She abandoned her husband

and joined the revolutionary struggle with her new lover. When Grothendieck was five, his mother left him in the hands of a Protestant pastor to travel to Spain and fight with the anarchists against Franco in defence of the Second Republic. After the Republican defeat, she took refuge with her husband in France and from there sent for her son. Johanna and Grothendieck were declared "undesirables" by the French government and sent, along with other "suspect foreign elements" who had formed part of the International Brigades, and other refugees from the Spanish Civil War, to the Rieucros camp, close to Mende, where Johanna contracted tuberculosis. By the time the war ended, Grothendieck was seventeen. He survived with his mother in extreme poverty picking grapes on the outskirts of Montpellier, the city where he began his studies. Mother and son had a close, aberrant relationship. Johanna died in 1957, of a relapse of tuberculosis.

When Grothendieck was still an undergraduate student at the University of Montpellier, his professor, Laurent Schwartz, gave him an article he had published not long before which included fourteen major unresolved problems, and asked Grothendieck to choose one of them for his thesis. The young man, who was always bored and distracted in his classes and seemed incapable of following instructions, returned three months later. Schwartz asked him which problem he had chosen and how far along he had got. Grothendieck looked at him, baffled. What did he mean by "which one"? He had solved all of them.

His talent caught the attention of everyone who met him, but it was difficult for him to find work in France. Because of his parents' constant displacements, Grothendieck had no nationality, and his only identity document was a Nansen passport, which classified him as "stateless".

He was physically imposing, tall, thin and athletic, with a square jaw, broad shoulders and a large, bull nose. The corners of his thick lips curved upwards, giving him a mischievous look, as though he were privy to a secret that everyone else did not even suspect. When he began to lose his hair, he shaved his head, a perfect oval. In photos, he looks like Michel Foucault's identical twin.

A talented boxer, fanatical about Beethoven's final quartets and Bach, he loved nature and venerated "the humble and long-lived olive tree, full of sun and life", but above all the things of this world, including mathematics, he had a devotion to writing that bordered on the fanatical. He wrote with such fervour that, in certain parts of his manuscripts, the pencil tip would pierce the page straight through. When calculating, he wrote his equations in his notebook and then retraced them over and over, until each symbol was so thick it was no longer intelligible, in thrall to the physical pleasure he felt by scratching graphite on paper.

In 1958, the French millionaire Léon Motchane built the Institute of Advanced Scientific Studies on the outskirts of Paris to serve Grothendieck's ambitions. There, Grothendieck, who had just turned thirty, announced a work programme that would re-establish the foundations of geometry and unify all the branches of mathematics. An entire generation of professors and students subjugated themselves to Grothendieck's dream. He would preach aloud while they took notes, expanded his arguments and wrote out drafts for him to correct. The most devout of all his collaborators, Jean Dieudonné, would get up at five in the morning, even if the sun had not yet risen, to review the transcripts from the previous day before Grothendieck burst into the classroom at eight on the dot, developing a fresh set of ideas that he had already begun debating with himself as he climbed the stairs of the institute. Grothendieck's seminar produced twelve volumes, more than twenty thousand pages that manage to bring together geometry, number theory, topology and complex analysis.

Unifying mathematics is a dream that only the most ambitious minds have pursued. Descartes was among the first to show that geometric forms can be described through equations. Whoever writes $x^2 + y^2 = 1$ is describing a perfect circle. Every possible solution to this basic equation represents a circle drawn on a plane. But if one considers not only real numbers and the Cartesian plane, but also the bizarre spaces of complex numbers, there appears a series of circles of various sizes that move as if they were living creatures, growing and evolving in time. Part of Grothendieck's brilliance was to recognize that there was something grander hidden behind every algebraic equation. He called this something a *scheme*. Each individual solution to an equation, each shape, was nothing but a shadow, an illusory projection that flashed forth from the general scheme, "like the contours of a rocky coast illuminated at night by the rotating lamp of a lighthouse".

Grothendieck was capable of creating an entire mathematical universe fit for a single equation. His *topoi*, for example, were seemingly infinite spaces that defied the limits of the imagination. Grothendieck compared them to "the bed of a river so vast and so deep that all the horses from all the kings of this world, and from all possible worlds, could drink from its waters together". To think in such terms demanded a completely novel conception of space, as radical as the change brought forth by Albert Einstein, fifty years before.

He loved choosing *le mot juste* for the concepts he discovered, as a way to tame them and render them familiar before he could fully grasp them. His *étales*, for example, evoke the calm, docile waves of a low tide, a still mirror of water, the surface of a wing stretched to breaking point, or the taut, white sheets swaddling a newborn child.

He was capable of sleeping at will, as many hours as he needed, then dedicating the whole of his energy to his work. He could begin working out an idea in the morning and not move from his desk until dawn the next day, squinting under the light of an old kerosene lamp. "It was fascinating to work with a genius," his friend Yves Ladegaillerie remembers. "I don't care for that word, but for Grothendieck there is no other. It was fascinating but also terrifying, because this was a man who simply did not resemble other human beings."

His capacity for abstraction seemed endless. He could make unexpected leaps to higher categories and work in orders of magnitude no one had dared to explore before. He formulated his ideas by removing one layer after the other, breaking down concepts, simplifying and abstracting until there seemed to be nothing left; there, in that apparent vacuum, he would discover the structures he had been searching for.

"My first impression on hearing him lecture was that he had been transported to our planet from an alien civilization in some distant solar system in order to speed up our intellectual evolution," a professor from the University of California at Santa Cruz said of him. Despite how radical they were, the mathematical landscapes Grothendieck conjured up gave no impression of artificiality. To the trained eyes of a mathematician, they revealed themselves as seemingly natural environments, for Grothendieck did not impose his will on things, preferring to let them grow and develop by themselves. The results had an organic beauty, as though each idea had budded and borne fruit following its own vital impulse.

In 1966, he won the Fields Medal, known as the Nobel of mathematics, but he refused to go to Moscow to receive it in protest against the imprisonment of the writers Yuli Daniel and Andrei Sinyavsky.

For two decades, his dominance was such that René Thom, another brilliant winner of the Fields Medal, admitted to having felt "oppressed" by Grothendieck's overwhelming technical superiority. Frustrated by his incapacity to rival Grothendieck's vertiginous output of groundbreaking ideas, Thom abandoned pure mathematics to develop catastrophe theory, a mathematical treatment that describes seven ways in which any dynamic system—be it a river, a tectonic fault or the fragile mind of a human being—can suddenly lose its equilibrium and collapse, falling into disorder and chaos.

"What stimulates me is not ambition or the thirst for power. It is the acute perception of something immense and yet very delicate at the same time." Grothendieck continued to push past the limits of abstraction. No sooner had he conquered new territory than he was preparing to expand its frontiers. The pinnacle of his investigations was the concept of *motive:* a ray of light capable of illuminating every conceivable incarnation of a mathematical object. "The heart of the heart" he called this strange entity located at the crux of the mathematical universe, of which we know nothing save its faintest glimmers.

Even his closest and most loyal collaborators believed he had gone too far. Grothendieck wanted to hold the sun in the palm of his hand, uncover the secret root that could bind together countless theories that bore no apparent relation to one another. They told him his goal was unattainable, and that his project sounded more like the pipe dreams of an amateur than a legitimate programme for scientific exploration. Grothendieck did not listen. After spending so long gazing down at the foundations of mathematics, his mind had stumbled into the abyss.

At the tail end of the Sixties, he travelled for two months to Romania, Algeria and Vietnam to give a series of seminars. One of the colleges at which he taught in Vietnam was later bombed by American troops; two professors and dozens of students died. When he returned to France, he was a changed man. Influenced by the clamour of the May '68 protests all around him, he called on more than a hundred students during a masterclass at the University of Paris in Orsay to renounce "the vile and dangerous practice of mathematics" in light of the hazards humanity was facing. It was not politicians who would destroy the planet, he told them, but scientists like them who were "marching like sleepwalkers towards the apocalypse".

From that day forward, he refused to participate in any maths conference that would not allow him to devote equal time to ecology and pacifism. During his talks, he gave away apples and figs grown in his garden and warned about the destructive power of science: "The atoms that tore Hiroshima and Nagasaki apart were split not by the greasy fingers of a general, but by a group of physicists armed with a fistful of equations." Grothendieck could not stop fretting over the possible effects that his own ideas could have on the world. What new horrors would spring forth from the total comprehension that he sought? What would mankind do if it could reach the heart of the heart?

In 1970, at the high point of his renown, creativity and influence, he resigned from the Institute of Advanced Scientific Studies after learning it accepted funds from the French Ministry of Defence.

In the following years, he abandoned his family, disavowed his friends, repudiated his colleagues, and fled the rest of the world.

"The great turning point" was the term Grothendieck used to describe the change in the direction of his life during his forties. All at once, he found himself swept up by the spirit of the age: he became obsessed by ecology, the military-industrial complex and nuclear proliferation. To his wife's despair, he founded a commune at home, where vagabonds, professors, hippies, pacifists, thieves, nuns and prostitutes dwelt side by side.

He became intolerant of all the comforts of bourgeois life; he tore up the carpets from the floors of his house, considering them superfluous adornments, and began to make his own clothing: sandals from recycled tires, trousers sewn from old burlap sacks. He stopped using his bed, instead sleeping on a door he had torn from its hinges. He only felt at ease among the poor, the young and the marginalized. The stateless, those without a homeland.

He was generous with his possessions and gave them away without a second thought. He was generous with those of others as well. One day, one of his friends, the Chilean Christian Mallol, arrived home with his wife after a dinner out to find his front door ajar, his windows open, the fireplace raging and the furnace blasting. Grothendieck was naked and asleep in his bath. Two months later, Mallol received a cheque for three thousand francs from Grothendieck, to cover the cost.

Although in general he was caring and kind, he could suffer sudden outbreaks of violence. During a pacifist protest in Avignon, he ran towards the containment barrier and knocked out two policemen who were attempting to impede the march, before being beaten to a pulp by dozens of officers who dragged him unconscious to the police station. At home, his wife heard him rant and rave while locked alone in his study, long monologues in German which degenerated into screams so loud that they shook the windows, followed by episodes of mutism that could last for days.

"Doing mathematics is like making love," wrote Grothendieck, whose sexual impulses rivalled his spiritual inclinations. Throughout his life he seduced both men and women. He had three children with his wife, Mireille Dufour, and two more outside his marriage.

He founded the group Survive and Live, devoting all of his resources and energy to it. He published a journal with a group of friends (though he wrote it practically on his own) to promote his ideas on self-sufficiency and care for the environment. He tried to involve those who had followed him in his mathematical undertakings, but no one shared his sense of urgency or could tolerate his extremism now that the object of his obsession was no longer the abstract world of numbers, but the concrete problems of society—which Grothendieck confronted with a degree of naivety that bordered on idiocy.

He was convinced that the environment had its own consciousness and that it was his duty to protect it. He would gather even the smallest shoots that grew between the cracks in the pavement outside his house to replant and care for them.

He began fasting once a week, then twice, and sometimes he would stop eating completely. Self-mortification became second nature to him. During a trip to Canada, he refused to wear shoes and walked through the snow in his sandals, like some Middle Eastern prophet spreading his gospel through a frozen desert. After a severe motorcycle accident, he declined anaesthesia, and agreed only to acupuncture during his surgery, as he had grown almost indifferent to physical pain. Behaviours of this kind fed the rumours that his critics spread to discredit him (and to defend themselves against the increasingly virulent charges Grothendieck levelled against them), the most outrageous of them all being that Grothendieck, in his zeal to reduce his impact on the planet, would shit in a bucket and then walk through the farms surrounding his home to spread his own excrement as fertilizer.

In 1973, the commune he had founded as a place open to all descended into pure lawlessness. First the police came to arrest two Japanese monks from the Order of the Marvellous Lotus Sutra who had overstayed their visas, and charged Grothendieck with harbouring illegal aliens. That same week, a girl he often spent the night with tried to hang herself with the curtains in his room. When he returned with her from the hospital, Grothendieck found the members of the commune dancing around an enormous bonfire they had built in the middle of the courtyard, feeding it with pages from his manuscripts. Grothendieck disbanded the community and retired to Villecun, a village of just a dozen tiny cottages.

In Villecun he lived without electricity or drinking water in a flea-infested cabin, but he was happier than he had ever been. He purchased a dilapidated hearse to get around, and, when the engine failed, he bought a second, even ricketier automobile with holes in the floorboard that opened onto the road, and drove it at the highest possible speed, though he had neither licence nor registration.

For five years, in almost total isolation, he devoted himself to manual labour, undertaking no major projects. His children did not visit him, he had no lovers, and he ignored all his neighbours with the exception of a twelve-year-old girl he helped with her arithmetic homework. When he had exhausted his savings, he began teaching mathematics at the University of Montpellier to cover the costs of his spartan existence. His undergraduate students could not have imagined that the man who received them dressed in rags like a vagrant, and whom they would find asleep on the classroom floor if they arrived early, was a living legend.

In Villecun, he focused his immense analytical powers on his own mind. The result was a change even more radical than the one that had drawn him away from mathematical research, a complete metamorphosis that he tried to encapsulate in a cryptic list tracing out the stations of his spiritual journey, which had taken him further and further away from common sense.

May 1933: longing for death
27–30 December 1933: birth of the wolf
summer (?) 1936: the Gravedigger
March 1944: existence of God the creator
June–Dec. 1957: call and betrayal
1970: the stripping away—entry into the mission
1–7 Apr. 1974: moment of truth, entry into the spiritual path
7 Apr. 1974: meeting with Nihonzan Myohoji, entry of the divine
July–Aug. 1974: insufficiency of the Law. I leave the paternal Universe
June–July 1976: awakening of the Ying
15–16 Nov. 1976: collapse of the image, discovery of meditation
18 Nov. 1976: re-encounter with my soul, entry of the Dreamer
August 1979–February 1980: I manage to meet my parents (imposture)
March 1979: discovery of the wolf
August 1980: meeting with the Dreamer—recovery of childhood
Feb. 1983–Jan. 1984: the new style ("In Pursuit of the Fields")
Feb. 1984–May 1986: Reaping and Sowing
25 Dec. 1986: the "sacrifice" of the ReS
*NB 25.12.1986: first erotico-mystic dreams
28 Dec. 1986: death and rebirth
1–2 Jan. 1987: mystico-erotic "abduction"

27 Dec. 1986–21 March 1987: metaphysical dreams,
   intelligence of dreams
8.1, 24.1, 26.2, 15.3 (1987): prophetic dreams
28.3.1987: nostalgia for God
30.4.1987— ... The Key to Dreams

Between 1983 and 1986, he wrote *Reaping and Sowing: Reflections and Testimonies from a Mathematician's Past,* an outlandish work that no one in France dared to publish. Over thousands of pages, replete with what one colleague described as "mathematical phantasmagorias", Grothendieck delves into his own psyche in an attempt to understand everything, revealing a vast and terrifying intellect stripped increasingly bare, precariously balanced between enlightenment and paranoia.

The ideas of *Reaping and Sowing* turn in circles. The author returns to the same arguments over and over again, aspiring to total precision. He examines what he has just written in order to discard or affirm it with redoubled force, attempting to fix his words in a definitive form, which they naturally resist. A single page contains brusque changes of perspective, theme and tone, the product of a mind struggling against the limits of meaning and attempting, for once, to bring all things into its purview: "A perspective is by nature limited. It offers us one single vision of a landscape. Only when complementary views of the same reality combine are we capable of achieving fuller access to the knowledge of things. The more complex the object we are attempting to apprehend, the more important it is to have different sets of eyes, so that these rays of light converge and we can see the One through the many. That is the nature of true vision: it brings together already known points of view and shows others hitherto unknown, allowing us to understand that all are, in actuality, part of the same thing."

He lived like a hermit, reading, meditating and writing. In 1988, he nearly died of starvation. He had come to identify completely with the French mystic Marthe Robin, who was afflicted with stigmata and survived for five decades eating nothing but consecrated wafers. Grothendieck tried to surpass the forty days of fasting Christ spent in the desert, and for months nourished himself on soup from the dandelions he picked in his front garden and around his home. His neighbours, used to seeing him wandering in the street picking these flowers, saved him from death, visiting him with cakes and homemade dishes, and not leaving until he agreed to eat them.

He came to believe dreams were not proper to human beings, but missives from an external entity he called *Le Rêveur*, who sent them to allow us to recognize our true identities. For more than two decades, he kept a log of his evenings—*The Key to Dreams*—which allowed him to understand the Dreamer's nature: *Le rêveur n'est autre que Dieu.*

In June 1991, he attempted to cut all ties to the world. He incinerated twenty-five thousand pages of personal writings, burned his portrait of his father and gave away his mother's death mask. He handed over his final investigations—the notes from his failed attempt to illuminate the *motive*, that dark heart beating in the furthest depths of mathematics— to his friend Jean Malgoire to donate to his alma mater, the University of Montpellier. This marked the beginning of a period of flight that would last for the rest of his life, as he moved from village to village, shunning the journalists and students who sought him out, and returned letters sent to him by his family and friends without even bothering to open them.

For more than a decade, no one knew where he was. It was said he had died, that he had lost his mind, that he had gone off into the depths of the forest so no one would find his remains.

After rambling through the south of France with no fixed address, he took refuge in the hamlet of Lasserre, in Ariège, in the shadow of the Pyrenees, less than an hour from the concentration camp where his father had spent his final months before being sent to die in the Nazi gas chambers. As a child, Grothendieck had escaped barefoot in the middle of the night from Rieucros, the camp where he and his mother were interned, with the firm intention of walking to Berlin to assassinate Hitler with his own hands. The guards found him five days later, unconscious and a step away from death, shivering inside a hollowed-out tree trunk.

He played the piano at night. His neighbours in Lasserre—who knew he did not tolerate visitors—were surprised to hear beautiful polyphonies coming from his home, as though in his seclusion he had learned Mongolian chant and could intone multiple notes simultaneously. Grothendieck explains the matter in his diaries: at nightfall, he is visited by a woman with two faces. He calls her gentle side Flora and her demonic side Lucifera. They sing together to oblige God to make himself manifest, but "he is silent, and when he speaks, he does so in a voice so soft that no one can understand it."

In 2001, these same neighbours saw smoke and fire rising up from his home. According to Alain Bari, the mayor of Lasserre, Grothendieck did everything possible to prevent the firemen from intervening, and begged them to let it burn.

In 2010, his friend Luc Illusie received a letter from Grothendieck containing his "Declaration of Non-Publication". In it, Grothendieck prohibits all future sales of his work and demands the withdrawal of all his writings from libraries and universities. He threatens any and all who try to sell, print or disseminate his texts, published or unpublished. He wishes to unmake his influence, to dissolve into silence, to erase the last trace of his existence. "Make it all disappear, at once!"

The American mathematician Leila Schneps was one of the few people Grothendieck had contact with in his final years. She spent months looking for him, travelling through all the villages where she suspected he had lived, an old photograph of him in hand, asking people if they had seen him, unaware of the extent to which his physical appearance had changed. Tired of walking, she spent several days sitting on a bench in front of the only organic market in the region, hoping to see Grothendieck appear, and finally she saw an old man buying green beans, in a monk's habit, leaning on a cane. His face was obscured inside his hood and his features hidden behind an unkempt beard, long as a wizard's, but she recognized his eyes.

She approached him cautiously, imagining the recluse would run as soon as he saw her, and was surprised by the kindness with which Grothendieck greeted her, although he explained at once that he did not wish anyone else to find him. Barely capable of containing her emotion, she told him that one of the conjectures he had devised in his youth had finally been solved. Grothendieck smiled faintly. He said he had lost all interest in mathematics.

They spent the afternoon together. Schneps asked him why he had isolated himself. Grothendieck told her he did not hate human beings, nor had he turned his back on the world. His isolation was neither an escape nor a rejection; he had done it for the protection of mankind. Grothendieck said that no one should suffer from his discovery, but he refused to explain what he meant when he spoke of "the shadow of a new horror".

For a few months, they exchanged letters. Schneps was interested in learning about the ideas he had developed in physics—rumoured to be the last thing he was working on before his retirement. Grothendieck said that he would tell her everything if she could answer one single question: what is a metre?

Schneps did not respond until some weeks later, and her reply was more than fifty pages long, but Grothendieck returned her envelope without opening it, just as he would all those that followed it.

Towards the end of his life, his point of view was so remote that he was only capable of perceiving totality. Of his personality, nothing but tatters remained, tenuous threads pulled apart by years of constant meditation. "I have an irrefutable and perhaps blasphemous sense that I know God more intimately than I do any other being in this world, even though He is an impenetrable mystery, infinitely vaster than any physical entity."

*

He died at Saint-Girons hospital on Thursday, November 13, 2014. The cause of death is still unknown; he asked that it never be divulged.

The lone testimony of his final days comes from a nurse who cared for him at the hospital. According to her, Grothendieck refused to see his family and received only a single visitor, a tall, timid Japanese man too shy to enter the room until she invited him in.

The man, whom the nurse remembered as handsome but slightly hunchbacked, spent five days sitting on the edge of the bed during visiting hours, bent over in a very uncomfortable posture to bring his ear as close as possible to the patient's mouth, all the while scribbling in a notebook. He stayed with Grothendieck until he took his final breath, never speaking, and remained beside his body until they came to take it to the morgue.

The same man, or someone very similar, was stopped two days later by the guards at the University of Montpellier. He had been found kneeling in front of the door to the room that contained the four boxes of papers Grothendieck had left to the university—wrinkled scraps and equations written on napkins, which Grothendieck had dismissed as "little more than scribbles"—on condition that they never be opened.

The guards discovered a book of matches in the man's hand and a small jar of lighter fluid in his pocket, but they did not call the police. They expelled him from the campus, imagining he was insane or suffered from a mental handicap of some kind, because he would not look up from the floor and insisted repeatedly—yet always in the softest of voices—that they must let him go, as he had a very important seminar to present in the Department of Mathematics.

When We Cease
to Understand
the World

"The more I reflect on the physical part of Schrödinger's equation, the more disgusting I find it ... What Schrödinger writes makes scarcely any sense. In other words, I think it's bullshit."

Letter from Werner Heisenberg to Wolfgang Pauli

Preface

In July 1926, the Austrian physicist Erwin Schrödinger travelled to Munich to present one of the strangest and most powerful equations that the human mind has ever created.

He had become an international superstar overnight for his discovery of a simple way to describe the interior workings of atoms. Using formulae similar to those employed to predict the movement of waves in air and water, Schrödinger had achieved something apparently impossible: he had reined in the chaos of the quantum world, illuminating the orbits of electrons around the nucleus with an equation so elegant, exquisite and bizarre that some did not hesitate to call it "transcendent".

Yet its greatest charm was neither its beauty nor the myriad natural phenomena it was capable of describing; what seduced the entire physics community was how it enabled them to visualize things taking place at the smallest levels of reality. For those whose ambition was to scrutinize matter down to its most basic constituents, Schrödinger's equation was a Promethean fire capable of dissipating the darkness of the subatomic realm, revealing a world that until then had been veiled with mystery.

Schrödinger's theory seemed to confirm that elementary particles behaved in a manner similar to waves. If indeed this was their nature, they would obey well-known laws, ones that all the physicists on the planet could accept.

All except one.

Werner Karl Heisenberg had been forced to beg for loans to attend Schrödinger's seminar in Munich, and after buying his train tickets he barely had money left to cover his room and board in a shabby student pension. But Heisenberg was not just anyone. He was only twenty-three, but his colleagues already considered him a genius, as he had been the first to formulate a series of rules explaining the same matters as Schrödinger, but six months before him.

Their two theories could not have been more opposed; while Schrödinger had needed only a single equation to describe virtually the whole of modern chemistry and physics, Heisenberg's ideas and formulae were exceptionally abstract, philosophically revolutionary, and so dreadfully complex that only a handful of physicists understood how to use them, and even they suffered headaches trying to solve the simplest problems.

At the conference in Munich there was not a single empty seat. Heisenberg had to listen to Schrödinger's presentation sitting on the stairs of the auditorium, biting his nails. He could not contain himself until the end. When Schrödinger had reached the midpoint of his talk, Heisenberg leapt up, walked to the chalkboard before the astonished eyes of all present, and shouted that electrons were not waves and that the subatomic world could never be visualized. "It is far stranger than you can imagine!" A hundred people hissed at him and jeered, so vehemently that Schrödinger himself had to intervene and plead that they let Heisenberg speak. But no one cared to listen to the young man who demanded they give up any mental image they had of the atom. No one was willing to look at things as he did. When Heisenberg began to fill the chalkboard with his objections to Schrödinger's theory, he was pushed up the stairs and thrown out of the room. He was asking for too much. Why should scientists have to abandon common sense to peer at the smallest scale of matter? Surely Heisenberg was driven by envy. After all, Schrödinger's ideas had completely eclipsed his own discovery, denying him his place in history.

But Heisenberg knew they were all wrong. Electrons were neither waves nor particles. The subatomic world was unlike anything they had ever known. Of this he was utterly certain, his conviction running so deep that he was incapable of putting it into words. Because something had been revealed to him. Something that defied all explanation. Heisenberg had glimpsed a dark nucleus at the heart of things. And if that vision was not true, had all his suffering been in vain?

I.

Night in Heligoland

A year before the Munich conference, Heisenberg had become a monster.

In June 1925, while he was working at the University of Göttingen, an allergic reaction to pollen had deformed his face so that he was no longer recognizable. His lips looked like a rotten peach with the skin ready to come off, his eyelids puffed up until he could barely see. Unable to tolerate even one more day of spring, he boarded a ship to travel as far as possible from the microscopic particles that were torturing him.

His destiny was Heligoland—the name translates as "holy land"—Germany's only outlying island, so dry and inclement that trees barely rise from the ground and not a single flower blossoms amid its stones. He spent the boat journey locked up in his cabin, nauseated and vomiting, and when he set foot on the red dust of the island, Heisenberg felt so miserable that it took great effort for him not to look at the sheer cliffs—which rose more than seventy metres over his head—as the most expeditious solution to the multiple physical and psychological afflictions that had beset him since he had resolved to decipher the mysteries of the quantum realm.

Unlike his colleagues, who were enjoying the new golden age of physics by exploring novel ideas and undertaking ever more complex and precise calculations, Heisenberg was tormented by what he considered a fundamental flaw in the groundwork of the discipline: the laws that had served so well for the macroscopic world since the time of Isaac Newton fell apart when applied to the interior of the atom. Heisenberg wished to understand what elementary particles were and to unearth the common root of all natural phenomena. But that singular obsession—which he pursued unbeknownst to his supervisor—was consuming him completely.

The woman who received him in the small hotel where he had reserved a room could hardly conceal her shock when she saw him. She insisted on calling the police, certain the young man had suffered a beating at the hands of some drunken sailor during his crossing. When Heisenberg managed to convince her that it was only his allergies, Frau Rosenthal swore she would care for him until he had recovered completely, and devoted herself to this task as though the physicist were her only son, bursting into his room at all hours and forcing on him a fetid, supposedly miraculous elixir which Heisenberg pretended to drink, suppressing his retches until he could spit it out the window when the woman had finally left him in peace.

During his first days in Heligoland, Heisenberg followed a strict regimen of physical activity: at dawn he would leap into the sea and swim until he had rounded the huge outcrop where, according to the owner of the hotel, Germany's greatest pirate treasure was hidden. Heisenberg only returned to the shore when he was completely exhausted, almost on the point of drowning. He had acquired this strange habit as a child, when he competed against his brothers to see who could swim more laps around the pond on his parents' property. Heisenberg confronted his research with that same dogged attitude, working for days in a trance, forgetting to eat or even sleep. If he did not achieve a satisfactory result, he would find himself on the brink of a nervous breakdown; if he did, he would fall into an exalted, almost religious ecstasy—a fleeting state to which his friends believed he was slowly growing addicted.

From the window of his hotel, he enjoyed an unobstructed view of the sea. Looking at the waves scudding outwards and getting lost on the horizon, he could not help but recall the words of his mentor, the Danish physicist Niels Bohr, who had once told him that a part of eternity lies in reach of those capable of staring, unblinking, at the sea's deranging expanses. The summer before, they had explored the hills surrounding Göttingen, and Heisenberg felt that it was only after those long walks that his scientific career had truly begun.

Bohr was a colossus in the world of physics. The only scientist to achieve a similar degree of influence during the first half of the twentieth century was Albert Einstein, who was as much his rival as his friend. In 1922, Bohr had already received the Nobel Prize, and he had a gift for discovering young talents and bringing them under his wing. Such was the case with Heisenberg: during their strolls in the mountains, he convinced the young physicist that, when discussing atoms, language could serve as nothing more than a kind of poetry. Walking with Bohr, Heisenberg had his first intuition of the radical otherness of the subatomic world. "If a mere particle of dust contains billions of atoms," Bohr said to him as they were scaling the massifs of the Harz range, "what possible way is there to talk meaningfully of something so small?" The physicist—like the poet—should not describe the facts of the world, but rather generate metaphors and mental connections. From that summer onwards, Heisenberg understood that to apply concepts of classical physics such as position, velocity and momentum to a subatomic particle was sheer madness. That aspect of nature required a completely new language.

During his Heligoland retreat, Heisenberg decided to pursue an exercise of radical restriction. What could *really* be known of all that occurred inside an atom? Each time an electron changes its energy level while circling the nucleus, it emits a photon, a particle of light. That particle can be registered on a photographic plate. And that is the only information that can be directly measured, the only light that emerges from the obscurity of the quantum realm. Heisenberg decided to turn away from everything else. He would derive the rules governing existence at that scale armed only with that meagre handful of data. He would rely on no concepts, no images, no models. Reality itself would dictate what could (and what could not) be said about it.

When his allergies abated, allowing him to return to work full time, he arranged these data in an endless series of tables and columns, forming a complex set of matrices. Like a child attempting to put together a puzzle after losing the box top, enjoying the pleasure of assembling the pieces but ignorant of its true design, he spent days ordering and reordering them; little by little, he began to make out subtle relations, ways of adding and multiplying these matrices that revealed a new, increasingly abstract form of algebra. He would play with these matrices while he walked the footpaths that snaked across the island with his eyes pinned to the ground and no idea of where he was going. Each step forward in his calculations drew him further from reality. As the operations he managed to carry out grew more complex, the more obscure his underlying reasoning became. What possible relation existed between those lists of abstract numbers and the concrete molecules forming the stones scattered at his feet? How could he arrive at something that resembled, if only a little, the contemporary idea of the atom, starting from his rows and tables more befitting a lowly accountant than a proper physicist? The nucleus as a little sun, with electrons orbiting around it like planets; Heisenberg loathed that infantile, simplistic image. In his vision of the atom, those mental representations vanished: the little sun was snuffed out, and the electron stopped spinning like a top and dissolved into a formless mist. All that remained were numbers. A landscape as sterile as that which separated the two ends of the island.

Bands of wild horses crossed it at a gallop, shaking the ground beneath their hooves. Heisenberg could not imagine how they survived in such a wasteland. He followed their tracks to a gypsum quarry and whiled away his time cracking open stones to see if he could find one of the fossils for which the island was famous all over Germany. He spent the rest of that afternoon throwing rocks into the abandoned quarry, where they would shatter into a thousand pieces, foreshadowing the violence the British would unleash on Heligoland after the end of the Second World War, when they piled up all their unused munitions, torpedoes and mines and detonated the most powerful non-nuclear explosion in history, right in the middle of the island. The shockwaves of Operation Big Bang shattered windows sixty kilometres away and crowned the island with a column of jet-black smoke three thousand metres high, pulverizing the hillside Heisenberg had scaled twenty years earlier to see the sunset.

When he was almost at the edge of the cliffs, a dense fog covered the island. Heisenberg decided to go back to his hotel, but when he turned he realized that the trail had vanished. He cleaned the lenses of his glasses and looked around, trying to find some reference point that would lead him safely away from the precipice. As the fog thinned, he thought he recognized a huge boulder he had tried to scale the afternoon before, but no sooner had he seen it when the mist enveloped him once more. He was utterly disoriented. Like any good alpinist, he knew dozens of stories of simple hikes that had ended in tragedy: one misplaced foot could break your skull. He tried to keep calm, but everything around him had changed: the wind howled, blowing dust up from the ground and stinging his eyes, and the sun could not penetrate the haze. The few things he could make out alongside his feet—a seagull's skeleton, the wrinkled wrapper of a cough drop—seemed strangely hostile. The cold gnawed at the skin of his hands, though only minutes before it had been so hot he had had to remove his coat. Unable to advance in any direction, he sat down and leafed through his notebook.

Everything he had done up to that point struck him as senseless. The restrictions he had imposed on himself were absurd: it was impossible to illuminate the atom by darkening it in such a manner. A wave of self-pity had begun to well up inside him when a gust of wind parted the fog, revealing the path down to the village. He jumped up and ran, but the fog returned as quickly as it had dispersed. I know where the trail is, he told himself, I just need to get a little closer, pay attention to the smallest details of my surroundings, ten metres to that broken stone, twenty to those shards of glass, a hundred to the twisted roots of that tree; but a single look around sufficed to convince him there was no way of knowing whether he was approaching the road or walking straight towards the abyss. He was about to sit down again when he heard a dull thundering all around him. The noise shook the earth and grew in intensity until the gravel at his feet began to dance as though it had come alive. He thought he could distinguish a group of swiftly moving shadows on the edge of his field of vision. It's the horses, he said to himself, trying to calm the pounding of his heart; it's just the horses running blind through the fog. But when he looked for them once the sky had fully cleared, he could not find a single hoofprint.

In the days that followed, he worked tirelessly, closeted in his room, not even stopping to brush his teeth, and he would have continued in that way had Frau Rosenthal not burst in and pushed him out, saying that the room had begun to stink of death. Heisenberg walked down to the port, sniffing at his own clothes. When was the last time he had changed his shirt? He walked staring at the ground, so intent on his efforts to avoid the glances of his fellow tourists that he almost ran into a young woman who was trying to get his attention. He had spent so long without talking to anyone save for the hotel's owner that it took him a moment to realize that the girl with the bright eyes and curly hair was trying to sell him a little token for the poor. Heisenberg reached into his pockets; he did not have a single mark to offer her. The young woman blushed and told him not to worry, but Heisenberg's heart sank in his chest. What was he doing on that godforsaken island? He gazed at the woman until she was surrounded by a group of drunken dandies strolling with their arms around their girlfriends, and he realized he was probably the only single man on the entire island. He turned away, and was overtaken by a feeling of uncontrollable strangeness. The shops along the promenade looked like carbonized ruins left behind by a massive firestorm. A multitude of strangers thronged around him, their skin charred by a fire only Heisenberg could see; small girls ran with their pigtails ablaze, couples laughed as they burned together like kindling on a funeral pyre, their arms interlaced, flames licking their bodies and stretching up into the heavens. Heisenberg walked away, trying to control the tremors in his legs, but a deafening shriek pierced his eardrums as a ray of light shot through the clouds and drilled a hole into his brain. He ran back to the hotel, practically blinded by the aura that heralded one of his migraines, trying to resist his nausea and the agonizing pain spreading from his forehead to his temples, which felt as if someone were trying to split his head in two. When he finally dragged himself upstairs and fainted over his bed, he was quivering from fever.

Although unable to keep down his food, he refused to give up his walks around the island. He would shit squatting down as if he were a dog marking its territory, and then root around for stones to cover his filth, imagining that at any moment someone might surprise him with his trousers around his ankles. He was convinced his hostess was poisoning him with the tonic she forced him to drink; the more weight he lost from the vomiting and diarrhoea, the bigger the spoonfuls she gave him. When he was no longer capable of climbing out of his bed (in which he could barely stretch out his legs), he put on as much of his clothing as he could fit over his body and covered himself with five blankets, pulling them up to his neck, intending to "burn out" the fever, a home remedy he had learned from his mother and to which he submitted without question, convinced that any discomfort was preferable to handing himself over to a doctor.

Sweating from head to toe, he spent the day memorizing the *West-Eastern Divan*, a book of poems by Goethe that a previous guest had left behind in his room. He read the poems aloud, over and over, and certain verses echoed from his room and through the empty hallways of the hotel, to the bafflement of the other guests, who heard them as if they were the whispers of a ghost. Goethe had written them in 1819, inspired by the Sufi mystic Khwāja Shams-ud-Dīn Muḥammad Ḥāfeẓ-e Shīrāzī, known simply as Hafez. The German genius encountered the great Persian poet of the fourteenth century in a bad translation published in his home country and came to believe he had received the book at the behest of the divinity. He identified with him so closely that his voice changed completely, melding with that of the man who had sung the glories of God and wine four hundred years before. Hafez had been a drunken saint, a mystic and a hedonist. He devoted himself to prayer, poetry and alcohol. When he turned sixty years old, he traced a circle in the desert sand, sat down in its centre, and swore not to rise until he had touched the mind of Allah, the one and only God, mighty and sublime. He spent forty days in silence, tormented by the sun and wind, and when he broke his fast with a cup of wine given to him by a man who had found him on the verge of death, he felt a second consciousness awaken within him, superimposing itself over his own. That other voice dictated more than five hundred poems to him, helping Hafez to become the pinnacle of Persian literature. Goethe also had help writing his *Divan*, but his inspiration was not divine, rather the wife of one of his friends, Marianne von Willemer. She was as fanatical an admirer of Hafez as Goethe himself, and they wrote the book together, revising the drafts in letters rife with eroticism, in which the German poet imagines biting her nipples and ejaculating in her mouth, while she dreams of sodomizing him, in spite of the fact that they met only once, and there is no evidence they were able to fulfil any of their fantasies. Marianne composed the songs to the East Wind in the voice of Suleika, lover of Hatem, but she kept her co-authorship a secret until the night before she died, reciting those same verses Heisenberg read aloud, quaking with fever: *Where is the colour that might tame the sky? / The grey mist leaves me blind / the more I look, the less I see.*

Heisenberg insisted on working on his matrices even when ill: while Frau Rosenthal covered him in cool compresses, hoping to lower his temperature, and tried to convince him to call a doctor, he would rant about oscillators, spectral lines and harmonically bound electrons, convinced he need only hold out a few more days for his body to overcome the illness and his mind to find the way out from the labyrinth in which he had imprisoned it. Although he could hardly turn the pages, he continued reading those verses of Goethe, and each of them seemed an arrow aimed directly at his breast: *I only treasure those who long for death / in flames love has embraced me / in ashes every image of my mind.* When he managed to fall asleep, Heisenberg would dream of dervishes spinning in the centre of his room. Hafez pursued them on all fours, drunk and naked, barking at them like a dog. He threw his turban at them, his glass of wine, then the empty jug, trying to dislodge them from their orbits. When he could not wake them from their trance, he pissed on them one by one, leaving a trace of yellow spots on the pale fabric of their tunics, a pattern in which Heisenberg thought he could glimpse the secret of his matrices. Heisenberg stretched out his hands to grab them, but the spots became a long chain of numbers that danced all around him, girdling his neck in a tightening circle until he was scarcely able to breathe. Those nightmares were a welcome respite from his erotic dreams, which grew more intense as his strength failed him, and made him stain his sheets like an adolescent. Though he tried to prevent Frau Rosenthal from changing them, she would not let a day pass without cleaning his room from top to bottom. The shame he felt was nearly unbearable, but Heisenberg refused to masturbate: he was convinced that all his body's energies must remain bottled up so that he might devote them to his work.

Most nights he fell prey to insomnia. In his delirium, his mind would establish strange connections that allowed him to achieve direct results, forgoing any intermediate steps. He felt his brain split in two: each hemisphere worked on its own, without needing to communicate with the other, and as a result his matrices violated all the rules of ordinary algebra and obeyed the logic of dreams, where one thing can be many: he was capable of multiplying two quantities together and obtaining different answers depending on the order in which he proceeded. Three times two was six, but two times three might be eight. Too weary to question himself, he continued working until he had reached the final matrix. When he solved it, he left his bed and ran around his room shouting, "Unobservable! Unimaginable! Unthinkable!"

until the entire hotel was awakened. Frau Rosenthal entered in time to see him collapse on the floor and recoiled at the stench of his soiled pyjama bottoms. When she managed to calm him, she put him back to bed and ran off to fetch a doctor, paying no attention to his complaints, as he was passing in and out of his hallucinations.

Sitting at the foot of his bed, Hafez offered him a glass of wine. Heisenberg took it and drank it in long gulps, letting it run over his beard and chest, before realizing it contained the blood of the poet, who was now masturbating furiously while bleeding from his wrists. *All this food and drink have made you fat and ignorant!* Hafez hissed. *But if you give up sleep and nourishment, you will have one more chance. Don't just sit there thinking. Go out and submerge yourself in God's sea! Wetting a single hair won't bring you wisdom. He who sees God doesn't doubt. His mind and his vision are pure.* Woozy and confused, Heisenberg tried to follow the ghost's instructions, but his fever had flared up again, and his teeth would not stop chattering. He recovered his lucidity only to feel the prick of a needle and to hear Frau Rosenthal crying on the doctor's shoulder while he assured her that everything would be all right, that it was nothing more than a badly neglected cold, yet neither of them could see Goethe there, straddling the corpse of Hafez, now drained of all its blood, and yet still capable of maintaining a glorious erection, which the German poet attempted to invigorate with his lips, like a man blowing on the embers of a dying fire.

Heisenberg woke in the middle of the night. His fever had broken and his mind was exceptionally clear. He stood up from the bed and dressed mechanically, feeling himself totally alienated from his body. He approached his desk, opened his notebook and saw that he had finished every one of his matrices, though he did not know how he had constructed half of them. He took his coat and walked out into the cold.

There were no stars in the sky, only clouds lit by the moon, but his eyes had become so used to darkness after long days shut away that he was able to proceed with absolute certainty. He followed the route towards the cliffs, immune to the cold, and when he reached the highest point of the island, he saw a soft glow over the horizon, even though dawn was hours away. The radiance came not from the sun, but from the earth itself, and Heisenberg thought that perhaps it was the glare of an enormous city, but he knew the nearest one was more than a hundred kilometres to the west. There was no way for that light to reach him, and yet he could see it. Sitting with his face exposed to the wind whipped up from the sea, he opened his notebook and reviewed his matrices, so nervous that he committed one error after another, and had to start over again from the beginning. When he proved that the first was coherent, he could feel his body again. During the second, his hand shook from the cold. His pencil left tiny marks on the paper above and below his calculations, as if he had resorted to the symbols of an unknown language. His matrices were all consistent: Heisenberg had modelled a quantum system based wholly on direct observation. He had replaced metaphors with numbers and discovered the rules governing the inner phenomena of atoms. His matrices allowed him to describe the location of an electron from one moment to the next, and how it would interact with other particles. He had replicated in the subatomic world what Newton had done for the solar system, using only pure mathematics, with no recourse to imagery. He had no idea how he had arrived at his results, but there they were, written in his own hand; if he was correct, science could not only understand reality but begin to manipulate it at its most basic level. Heisenberg thought of the consequences knowledge of this nature might have, and was struck with a feeling of vertigo so profound that he had to restrain the impulse to throw his notebook into the sea. He felt he was looking past atomic phenomena towards a new sort of beauty. Too agitated to sleep, he walked towards a boulder jutting directly over the water. He climbed to the top, and sat down to wait for the sunrise with his legs dangling over the edge, listening to the waves beating against the rocks down below.

On returning to the University of Göttingen, Heisenberg fought to shape his epiphany into a publishable article. The final paper struck him as flimsy, if not downright absurd. Its pages spoke of neither orbits nor trajectories, of positions nor velocities; all of that had been replaced by a complex web of numbers governed by a set of mathematical rules so convoluted as to appear repulsive. The simplest calculation required a titanic effort, and, even for him, it was practically impossible to decipher the connection between his own matrices and the real world. And yet they worked. Too insecure to publish the paper, he handed it to Niels Bohr, who left it on his desk for weeks.

The Dane began to leaf through it one morning when he had nothing better to do, then reread it again and again, his fascination growing all the while. Soon Heisenberg's new discovery occupied his mind so fully that it kept him up at night. What the young German had achieved had no precedents: it was like deducing all the rules of Wimbledon— the number of sets, the length of the grass, the tension of the nets and even the mandatory white that players have to wear—from the few balls that flew out of the stadium, without ever having witnessed what takes place on the court. Hard as he tried, Bohr could not tease out the strange logic that Heisenberg had employed in the creation of his matrices, but he knew the young man had hit on something fundamental. The first thing he did was notify Einstein: "Heisenberg's latest paper, soon to be published, appears rather mystifying but is certainly true and profound and will have enormous implications."

In September 1925, Heisenberg published "On a Quantum-Theoretical Reinterpretation of Kinematic and Mechanical Relations", in Issue 33 of the *Zeitschrift für Physik*, the first formulation of quantum mechanics.

II.

The Prince's Waves

Heisenberg's ideas left people stupefied.

Although Einstein himself took to the study of "matrix mechanics" as if it were a map to a buried treasure, there was something about the ideas of the young German physicist that he found truly repulsive. "Heisenberg's theory is the most interesting of all recent contributions," he wrote to his friend Michele Besso, "a devilish calculation that incorporates infinite determinants and uses matrices instead of coordinates. It's quite brilliant. And its cursed complexity insulates it from being easily disproven." But what Einstein abhorred was not the formulae's hermeticism, but something far more important: the world Heisenberg had discovered was incompatible with common sense. Matrix mechanics did not describe normal, albeit unimaginably small objects, but an aspect of reality that concepts of classical physics could not even name. For Einstein, this was not a minor problem. The father of relativity was a great master of visualization: all of his ideas about space and time had been born of his capacity to imagine himself in the most extreme physical circumstances. For this reason, he was unwilling to accept the restrictions demanded by Heisenberg, who seemed to have gouged out both his eyes in order to see further. Einstein sensed that if one followed that line of thinking to its ultimate consequences, darkness would infect the soul of physics: if Heisenberg triumphed, a fundamental aspect of the laws that governed the physical world would remain forever obscure, as if chance had somehow nested in the heart of matter and become inextricably bound to its most fundamental constituents. Someone had to stop him. Someone had to smash the box in which Heisenberg had trapped the atom. And for Einstein, that someone was a peculiar young Frenchman, as shy as he was extravagant: Prince Louis-Victor Pierre Raymond, 7th duc de Broglie.

Scion of one of France's most illustrious dynasties, de Broglie grew up pampered by his elder sister, Princess Pauline, who adored him above all others, and described him in her memoirs as a slight, slender boy "with curly hair like a poodle, a small, cheery face, and eyes full of malice". During his childhood, little Louis enjoyed a life of privilege and luxury, but was thoroughly ignored by his parents. His sister compensated for this lack of affection, and celebrated his every fancy: "He talked non-stop at the dining room table, and was incapable of holding his tongue, however much they yelled at him—and his remarks were irresistible! Raised in solitude, he had read a great deal and lived in a completely unreal world. He had a prodigious memory, and could recite entire scenes of classical theatre with inexhaustible flair, but he trembled in the most innocuous circumstances: pigeons terrified him, he was afraid of cats and dogs, and the sound of our father's shoes climbing the stairs could send him into a panic." As the boy showed a particular liking for history and politics (at just ten years old, he could recite the names of all the ministers of the Third Republic), his family presumed he would pursue a career in diplomacy, but he was soon seduced by the laboratory of his older brother, the experimental physicist Maurice de Broglie.

The laboratory took up the better part of one of his family's mansions, and grew until it occupied an entire corner of Rue de Chateaubriand. In the stables where the thoroughbred horses had once slept, enormous X-ray generators now hummed, connected to the main laboratory via thick cables that ran through the porcelain in the guest bathroom and the priceless Gobelin tapestries that covered the walls of Maurice's studio. The older brother had been left in charge of the little prince upon their father's death. De Broglie began his scientific studies, and showed the same aptitude for the theoretical branch of physics that his brother Maurice had shown for the experimental. Still a student, he happened on the notes on quantum physics his brother had taken as secretary of the first Solvay Conference, the most prestigious scientific gathering in Europe. This apparently fortuitous event not only altered the course of his life, but even provoked an extraordinary change in his character, so that his sister Pauline hardly recognized him when she returned from her vacations in Italy: "The *petit prince* who entertained me throughout my childhood had entirely vanished. Now he lived in permanent isolation in a small room, immersed in a mathematics manual and chained to a repetitive and inflexible routine. With frightening speed, he had turned into an austere man leading a monastic life, and his right eyelid, which had always drooped a bit over his eye, now covered it almost completely, spoiling his looks in a way I deplored, as it accented his absent and effeminate air."

In 1913, de Broglie made the horrific mistake of enlisting in the corps of engineers to fulfil his obligatory military service, unaware that just a couple of months later the First World War would break out. He would serve as a telegraph operator in the Eiffel Tower until the end of the conflict, maintaining the instruments used to intercept enemy messages. By nature a coward and a pacifist, de Broglie found army life more than he could bear, and in the years following the war he would complain bitterly of the effects of the European conflict on his mind, which, according to him, was never the same again.

The only one of his brothers in arms with whom he maintained relations was a young artist, Jean-Baptiste Vasek, de Broglie's first true friend since his infancy, whose company had been his only source of amusement during the years of tedium they spent together up in the tower. After they were discharged, their friendship remained close and affectionate. Vasek was a painter, but he had also compiled an extensive collection of works he called *art brut*: poems, sculptures, drawings and paintings composed by psychiatric patients, mentally disabled children, drug addicts, alcoholics, perverts and sexual deviants, whose twisted visions, it seemed to him, bore the seeds from which the myths of the future would spring forth. De Broglie was never convinced of the possible utility of what Jean-Baptiste called "creative energy in its purest state", but his dedication to art resembled Louis's own monomaniacal devotion to physics, and they could spend whole afternoons conversing in one of the salons in de Broglie's mansion, or else in tranquil silence, neither feeling the passage of time nor paying attention to what was occurring in the outside world.

De Broglie only realized how deeply he had fallen in love with his friend when the painter committed suicide. Vasek left no explanation for what he had done, just a note in which he begged his "dearest Louis" to guard his collection and, if at all possible, to continue building it, a final wish that Louis followed to the letter.

De Broglie abandoned his physics studies and focused his extraordinary willpower and considerable resources on continuing the project of his departed love. Using a part of his family inheritance, he visited all the asylums in France and many more across the continent, and bought whatever sort of art the patients were capable of making. Not only did he accept works already completed, he offered money in exchange for new pieces, bringing materials to the hospital directors and easing any resistance with bribes in cash or jewels from his mother's collection. Nor did he stop there: when he had plundered the asylums, he established a foundation to work with children stricken with developmental difficulties, and, when he had exhausted the supply of children, he funded a scholarship for violent prisoners and sex offenders. Finally, he approached the Catholic charities and financed a home for beggars that would offer them food and lodging in exchange for a poem, a drawing or a musical score. Once he had filled the palace where the works were stored, and there was no room for another single piece of paper, he announced a grand exhibition, "La Folie des Hommes", attributing its curatorship to his friend.

The inauguration brought together such a crowd that policemen had to disperse the onlookers who gathered at the gates of the property to prevent anyone from being crushed. The opinion of the critics was divided, with two irreconcilable factions: those who denounced the utter decadence the artistic world had plunged into, and those who applauded the birth of a new kind of art that made the experiments of the Dadaists look like parlour games for indolent poseurs. Even in a country like France, habituated to the eccentricities of what remained of its nobility, the exhibition was incomprehensible, and the rumour that Prince de Broglie had squandered his family fortune to pay homage to one of his lovers was on the lips of everyone in high society at that time. When de Broglie read an article that pitilessly mocked Jean-Baptiste's paintings (which he had shown in a special room within the exhibition), he locked himself away in the building with the works of all the madmen in Europe, and for three months saw no one but his sister, who brought him dishes of food he would leave untouched outside the door.

Convinced that Louis's intent was to let himself die from hunger, Pauline begged their older brother to intervene. Maurice beat on the door of the palace for twenty minutes without receiving a response, then returned and blew open the lock with a shotgun. He came in accompanied by five servants, ready to drag his brother off to a sanatorium, and strode shouting through the halls and rooms with their statues of rubbish, seeing for the first time the hellish scenes drawn in crayon, until he reached the main exhibition hall, where there was a perfect replica of the cathedral of Notre Dame—down to the features of its smallest gargoyle—wrought entirely in human faeces. Furious, he quickened his pace until he reached the bedroom on the top floor, where he had expected to find little Louis filthy and malnourished, if not dead, and was surprised to see him clad in a velvet suit, moustache and hair recently trimmed, smoking a thin cigarette with an immense smile across his face and his eyes beaming as they had when he was a child.

"Maurice," de Broglie said, handing him a bundle of papers as naturally as if they had spent the afternoon together, "I need you to tell me if I've lost my mind."

Two months later, Louis de Broglie presented the ideas that would win him his place in history. They were contained in his doctoral dissertation, which he entitled, with characteristic modesty, *Research on the Theory of the Quanta*. He defended it before an absolutely baffled jury from the university, in a monotonous tone that almost put them to sleep, and left the room without knowing if he was to be awarded his degree, as those meant to evaluate him were completely unable to grasp what they had just heard.

"Physics in its contemporary state contains false doctrines that exercise a dark influence on our imagination," de Broglie declared in his high-pitched, nasal voice. "For more than a century, we have divided earthly phenomena into two fields: atoms and particles of solid matter on the one hand, and the intangible waves of light, propagated through the sea of the luminous ether, on the other. But these two systems cannot remain separate; we must bring them together in a single theory that explains their multiple interactions. Our colleague Albert Einstein has taken the first step in this direction; twenty years ago now, he postulated that light is not simply a wave, but contains particles of energy; these photons, which are nothing more than concentrated energy, travel within the waves of light. Many have doubted this idea's veracity; others have tried to close their eyes so as not to see the new path forward it reveals to us. Because—let us not be mistaken—this is an incontestable revolution. We are talking here about the most precious object in physics, light, which allows us not only to see the forms of this world, but shows us the stars that adorn the spiral arms of the galaxy and the hidden heart of matter. But this object is not singular—it is double. Light exists in two different ways. Thus, it transcends all the categories with which we have tried to encapsulate the myriad forms of nature. As wave and as particle, it inhabits two distinct orders and is possessed of identities as opposed as the two faces of Janus. Like that Roman god, it expresses the contradictory properties of what is discrete and what is continuous, what is local and what is spread out. Those opposed to this revelation argue that accepting such a novel orthodoxy demands a departure from reason. To them I say the following: all matter is possessed of such dualism! Not only light but each of the atoms with which the godhead has constructed the universe is subject to this twofold nature. The thesis you hold in your hands makes plain that for each particle of matter—electron or proton— there exists an associated wave that transports it through space. I realize many of you will doubt my reasoning. I confess that it is the fruit of solitude. I admit its character is bizarre, and I accept whatever calumny may come to me if it is shown to be false. And yet today I say to you with absolute certainty that all things can exist in two ways, and that nothing is as solid as it appears; the stone in the child's hand, which he aims at the idle sparrow on its branch, could run like water between his fingers."

De Broglie had lost his mind.

When Einstein proposed the "particle-wave duality" in 1905, everyone thought he had gone too far. But light is immaterial, his critics reasoned, so perhaps it can exist in this strange form. Matter, on the other hand, was solid. That it should behave like a wave was inconceivable. The two things could not be more opposed. A particle of matter, in the end, is like a tiny grain of gold: it exists in a determinate space and occupies only that one place in the world. Its precise location can be ascertained from one minute to the next, because its matter is concentrated. For this same reason, such a body propelled forwards will bounce back if it encounters an obstacle, and will always land at a specific point. Waves, on the other hand, are like the waters of the sea, grand and capacious, outstretched along an endless surface, and, in this way, exist in multiple positions simultaneously: if a wave crashes against a rock, it can surround it and continue on its way. If two come into contact from opposite directions, they may counteract each other and dissipate or else continue on their same path unaffected. And when a wave breaks on the coast, it strikes numerous places on the beach, not all at the same time. The two phenomena are in essence opposed, contradictory, their behaviour antagonistic, and yet, according to de Broglie, all atoms were—like light—both wave and particle, at times acting like the first, at times like the second.

De Broglie's affirmations were so incongruous with the received wisdom of his age that the jury was uncertain how to evaluate his proposal. Rarely did a doctoral thesis oblige them to conceive of matter in a radically new way. Their ranks included three luminaries from the Sorbonne—the Nobel Prize-winning physicist Jean Baptiste Perrin, the renowned mathematician Élie Cartan and the crystallographer Charles-Victor Maugin—as well as Paul Langevin, an invited professor from the Collège de France. But none of them could understand young de Broglie's revolutionary ideas. Maugin refused to accept the existence of waves of matter; Perrin wrote to Maurice de Broglie, who was anxious to know whether Louis had obtained his doctorate, confessing that "all I can tell you is your little brother is very intelligent." Nor did Langevin know what to say, and he sent a copy of the dissertation to Albert Einstein to see whether the pope of physics was capable of grasping what the prim Frenchman had proposed.

Einstein did not respond.

When months had passed, Langevin worried his message had been lost in the post. Under pressure from the Sorbonne, which demanded a definitive verdict, he sent a second letter to inquire whether Einstein had found the time to read the thesis and whether any of it made sense to him.

His answer arrived two days later, and meant the immediate consecration of de Broglie, whose work Einstein saw as the beginning of a new way forward for physics: "He has lifted a corner of the great veil. This is the first weak beam of light to penetrate the dilemma of the quantum world, the most terrible of our generation."

III.

Pearls in His Ears

A year later, de Broglie's dissertation reached the hands of a brilliant but failed physicist in whose mind the waves of matter grew to monstrous proportions.

In the interwar period, Erwin Rudolf Josef Alexander Schrödinger suffered many of the afflictions that plagued Europe as a whole: he went bankrupt, fell ill with tuberculosis, and in a matter of years had lived through the decline and death of his father and grandfather, along with a series of personal and professional humiliations that had ruined a once promising career.

By comparison, the Great War had been relatively calm for him. In 1914, he joined the Austro-Hungarian army as an officer and was sent to command a small artillery unit on the plains of Veneto. Schrödinger left for Italy armed with two pistols he had paid for from his own pocket, but he never had occasion to use them. He was transferred to a fortress in the mountains of Alto Adige in the north of the country, where he enjoyed the fresh highland air while two thousand metres below him countless soldiers had begun to dig the trenches they would die in.

His only real moment of fright took place during the ten days he spent as a lookout in one of the towers of the fortress.

Schrödinger fell asleep gazing at the stars, and, when he awoke, he saw a trail of lights advancing over the mountainside. He leapt up and calculated, based on the stretch of land they occupied, that they were a force of at least two hundred men—three times larger than his own company. He was so afraid of engaging in real combat that he ran from one side of the room to the other, unable to recall what sort of alarm he was supposed to sound. When he went to ring the bell, he realized the lights were perfectly still, and when he spied them through his binoculars he saw they were Saint Elmo's Fire: flickers of plasma that enveloped the tips of the barbed wire surrounding the fortress, which were charged with static electricity from an approaching storm. Utterly bewitched, Schrödinger gazed at the blue lights until the last of them vanished, and, for the rest of his life, he would pine for that strange luminescence.

He spent the war with no occupation for his mind, awaiting orders that did not come and filling out reports no one read, until he fell into a state of extreme apathy. His staff complained that Schrödinger would not rise before lunchtime and then took naps that lasted the entire afternoon. He felt groggy throughout the day and could not bear to remain standing for more than five minutes at a time. He seemed to have forgotten the names of his comrades, as though a poisonous, corrosive miasma had invaded his mind. Although he tried to use the dead hours to page through the physics articles his colleagues sent him from Austria, he was incapable of concentrating; one thought ran into the next, and he had the sense that the tedium of war was spawning a long-dormant psychosis in him. "Sleep, eat, play cards. Sleep, eat, play cards. Is this a life?" he wrote in his diary. "I no longer ask myself when the war will be over. I ask whether it is at all possible for a thing such as this to end." When Germany signed the armistice in November 1918, Schrödinger returned to a Vienna besieged by hunger.

In the years to come, he saw the world in which he had grown up crumble apart: the emperor was deposed, Austria became a republic, and his mother lived out the final years of her life in wretched penury, her body consumed by the cancer that had taken root in one of her breasts. Schrödinger was unable to save his family's linoleum factory, which shut down as a result of the economic blockade the English and French upheld even after the cessation of hostilities. The victorious powers watched unmoved as the Austro-Hungarian Empire disintegrated and millions of people struggled to survive without nourishment or coal to stay warm through winter. The streets of Vienna filled with mutilated soldiers who had brought back with them the spectres of the battlefield; their nerves, damaged by gas in the trenches, twisted their faces into ghoulish grimaces, spasms shook their muscles, rattling the medals that hung from their tattered uniforms and making them chime like the bells in a leper colony. Control of the population was left in the hands of an army whose soldiers were as weak and famished as those they were meant to govern; fat white maggots infested their rations of meat, less than a hundred grams per person per day. When the troops distributed what little foodstuffs arrived in their country from Germany, total chaos ensued: during one of the disturbances, Schrödinger watched the mob knock a policeman from his horse. In five minutes, the beast was dismembered by a hundred women, who flocked around the cadaver to tear away the very last strips of its flesh.

Schrödinger himself got by on the miserable salary he earned from giving occasional classes at the University of Vienna. The rest of the time he had nothing to do. He devoured the writings of Schopenhauer, through whom he came to know the philosophy of Vedanta, and he learned that the horrified eyes of the mutilated horse in the square were also the eyes of the policeman mourning its death; that the teeth that bit into the raw meat were the same that had champed at the grass in the hillside pastures, and that when the women had torn the immense heart from the animal's chest with their hands, it was their own blood that slathered their faces, because every individual manifestation is only a reflection of Brahman, the absolute reality that underlies the phenomena of the world.

In 1920, he married Annemarie Bertel, but the abundant happiness of the lovers' early days failed to survive the reality of marriage. Schrödinger could not find decent work, and his wife earned more in one month as a secretary than he did in a year as a professor. He made her resign, and became an itinerant physicist, travelling from one poorly paid post to the next with his wife in tow: they went from Jena to Stuttgart, from Stuttgart to Breslau, and from there on to Switzerland. His luck seemed to change when he was named head of theoretical physics at the University of Zurich, but after one semester he had to stop teaching following a violent attack of bronchitis, later revealed to be the first signs of tuberculosis. He was forced to spend nine months in the clear air of the mountains, interned with his wife in the sanatorium of Doctor Otto Herwig in Arosa in the Swiss Alps. He would return in later years whenever his pulmonary health declined. That first time, Schrödinger weathered the high-altitude cure in the shadows of the Weisshorn and made an almost complete recovery, except for a strange after-effect none of the doctors could explain: he developed a hypersensitivity to sound bordering on the supernatural.

In 1923, Schrödinger was thirty-seven years old, and had at last established a comfortable routine in Switzerland. He and Anny took numerous lovers, but each tolerated the other's infidelities, and they lived together in peace. His only torment was the knowledge that he had wasted his talents. His intellectual superiority had been evident since childhood: at school, he had always had the highest mark in every subject. His schoolmates were used to Erwin knowing absolutely everything, so that decades later one of them would still remember the only question a teacher had ever posed to which young Schrödinger had not known the answer: what is the capital of Montenegro? His reputation as a genius followed him to the University of Vienna, where his undergraduate colleagues referred to him as The Schrödinger. His hunger for knowledge extended to all areas of science, including biology and botany; moreover, he was obsessed with painting, theatre, music, philology and the study of Classics. His teachers predicted a glorious future for him, on account of his irrepressible curiosity and his evident talent in the exact sciences, but several years after graduating, The Schrödinger found himself nothing more than a run-of-the-mill physicist. None of his articles had made a significant contribution to the field. He had no siblings, nor could he have children with Anny, and if he died, his family name would be lost forever. His biological and intellectual sterility made him consider divorce: perhaps he should give up everything, perhaps he should stop drinking and chasing after every woman he met, or leave physics behind and pursue another of his passions. Perhaps, perhaps. He spent the best part of a year thinking about it, but the result was nothing but increasingly violent arguments with his wife, aggravated by her intense affair with the Dutch physicist Peter Debye, one of Schrödinger's colleagues from the University of Zurich. With nothing to look forward to but a grey, repetitive future, Schrödinger fell into the same apathy that had ravaged him during the war.

In this state, he received an invitation from his dean to present a seminar on the ideas of de Broglie. He accepted the task with an enthusiasm he had not known since his student days. He analysed the Frenchman's work front and back, and recognized immediately, just as Einstein had, the potential in the prince's thesis. At last, Schrödinger had found something to sink his teeth into, and he preened himself during his presentation before the assembled physics department as if he were presenting his own ideas. He explained that quantum mechanics, which was causing such an uproar, could be brought under the purview of a classical schema. There was no need to change the groundwork of the discipline to probe matters at quantum level—no need of one physics for large things and another for small. "And spare us any resort to the repulsive algebra of that accursed *Wunderkind*, Werner Heisenberg!" Schrödinger said to them, provoking a fit of laughter among his colleagues. If de Broglie was right, all atomic phenomena shared one attribute, and might even—Schrödinger postulated—be nothing more than individual manifestations of an eternal substrate. He was about to finish his remarks when Debye cut him off. That manner, he said, of conceiving of waves was rather childish. It was one thing to say that matter consisted of waves and another, very different one to explain *how* they undulated. If Herr Schrödinger wished to speak with a modicum of rigour, he would need a wave equation. Without it, de Broglie's theory was like the French monarchy itself, as charming as it was useless.

Schrödinger returned home with his tail between his legs. Debye may have been right, but his comment was crude, pedantic and malicious. He had always detested that goddamned Dutchman. It was enough seeing how he looked at Anny. Not to mention how she looked at him . . . "Son of a bitch!" he screamed, shut up in his studio. *Leck mich am Arsch! Friss Scheiße und krepier!* He kicked over his furniture and threw his books against the wall until a coughing fit brought him to his knees. He fell over panting, his face inches from the wooden floor, his handkerchief stuffed in his mouth as he heaved and retched. When he took it out, he saw a large bloodstain, like a rose with opened petals, an unequivocal sign that his tuberculosis had returned.

Schrödinger arrived at the sanatorium at Villa Herwig shortly before Christmas, and swore he would not return to Zurich without an equation to shove in Debye's face.

He moved into the same room he always took, next to the daughter of the director, Doctor Herwig, who had divided the sanatorium into one wing for critical patients and another for cases like Schrödinger's. The doctor had raised his adolescent daughter on his own after his wife died from complications while giving birth. The girl had suffered from tuberculosis since the age of four, and her father blamed himself for her misfortune: she had grown up crawling between the legs of the diseased. The girl had seen hundreds of people die, affected by the same illness as her own, and perhaps it was for this reason that she radiated a supernatural calm, a diaphanous, other-worldly air only broken in those moments when the bacteria awakened in her lungs. Then she would walk through the halls of the centre, her dress spotty with blood, her collarbones stark against her slight shoulders as if about to tear through the skin, like the velvet antlers of a deer during their summer growth.

The first time Schrödinger saw her, the girl had been only twelve years old, but, even then, he had found her stunning. In this, he was no different from the rest of the patients, who were enchanted by this strange creature and seemed to coordinate their cycles of illness and remission with those of little Miss Herwig. For her father, this was one of the oddest phenomena he had encountered in the course of his career, and he sought comparisons for it in the animal kingdom, from the synchronized flight of starlings to the orgiastic outbursts of cicadas and the sudden metamorphosis of locusts—solitary, gentle insects whose proportions and character are deformed until they constitute an insatiable plague, capable of devastating an entire region before dying en masse, fertilizing the ecosystem with such an excess of nutrients that the doves, crows, ducks, ravens and magpies devour them until they are no longer capable of taking flight. If his daughter was healthy, the doctor could rest assured that he would lose not a single one of his patients; if she was ill, he knew he would soon have empty beds. The girl herself had been close to dying more than once. Her condition could transform her over the course of a single night: she lost so much weight that she seemed to have shrunk to half her size, her blonde hair turned thin like that of a newborn, and her skin, which was normally as pale as a cadaver's, became practically transparent. That coming and going between the worlds of living and dead had deprived the girl of the pleasures of childhood, but endowed her with a wisdom far greater than her years. Lying in bed for months, she had read not only all the scientific volumes in her father's library, but also the books left behind by patients who had been discharged, and others she received as gifts from the chronic cases. Her eclectic reading and constant isolation had produced an unusually alert mind and an insatiable curiosity; during Schrödinger's previous visit, she had assailed him with questions about the most recent advances in theoretical physics, about which she seemed to be thoroughly informed, despite having had virtually no contact with the outside world and never having ventured beyond the region surrounding the sanatorium. At just sixteen years old, Herwig had the mind, the bearing and the presence of someone much older. Schrödinger was quite the opposite.

Now close to forty, he retained his youthful appearance and his adolescent attitude. Unlike his colleagues, he cultivated an informal demeanour, and typically dressed more like a student than a professor. This caused him more than a few problems: once, the concierge of a Zurich hotel refused to admit him to the room booked in his name, convinced he was a vagabond; another time, security guards tried to deny him entry to a prestigious scientific conference to which he had been invited after seeing him arrive with dust in his hair and a crust of mud on his shoes from crossing the mountain on foot instead of taking the train like a respectable citizen. Doctor Herwig knew perfectly Schrödinger's unconventional character, how he often brought his lovers into the sanatorium, and yet (or perhaps for that very reason) he respected him enormously, and, whenever Schrödinger's health allowed it, they would ski for hours at a time or climb the nearby mountains together. The physicist's stay this time had coincided with the doctor's desire that his daughter finally develop a social life of her own, to which end he had registered her at the most prestigious girls' school in Davos—but she had failed the mathematics section of the entrance examination. As soon as Schrödinger set foot in the clinic, the doctor took him aside, asking him if he might devote a few hours to tutoring his daughter, if, of course, his health and his professional obligations allowed. Schrödinger refused in the most cordial way possible, then ran upstairs, taking the steps two by two, driven by something that had begun to take shape in his imagination the minute he breathed in the rarefied alpine air, a spell that he knew any distraction, however slight, could vanquish.

He entered his room and sat at the desk without removing his coat or hat. He opened his notebook and began to sketch out his ideas, first slowly and without organization, then at a manic speed, with greater and greater concentration, until everything around him seemed to disappear. He worked for hours, not getting up from his chair, with a tingle running down his spine, and only when the sun had emerged over the horizon and he was too tired to see the paper before him did he drag himself off to bed, falling asleep with his shoes on.

When he awoke, he did not know where he was. His lips were cracked and there was a buzzing in his ears. His head throbbed as though from a hangover after a long night of drinking. He opened the window to let the cool air refresh him, then settled down at his desk, anxious to review the fruit of his epiphany. When he glanced at his notes, his stomach turned. What was this nonsense? He read them from front to back, then from back to front, but nothing written there made sense to him. He failed to understand his own reasoning, how one step led to the next. On the last page, he found the draft of an equation similar to the one he had been looking for, but it bore no apparent relation to the pages that had come before. It was as if someone had entered his room while he slept and had left these calculations there, an unsolvable riddle, just to torture him. What had felt, the night before, like the most significant intellectual transport of his life now seemed little more than the frenzy of an amateur physicist, a sorry episode of megalomania. He rubbed his temples to try and calm his nerves and distance himself from the image in his mind of Debye and Anny laughing at him, but, still, he remained forlorn. He threw his notebook against the wall so hard that the pages tore away from the spine and flew across the room. Disgusted with himself, he changed his clothes, walked with a crestfallen expression to the canteen, and sat in the first empty chair he found.

When he called over the waiter to ask for a coffee, he realized he had arrived during the mealtime of the chronically ill.

Looking at the old woman sitting in front of him, he noticed first her long fingers, sculpted by centuries of wealth and privilege, holding a cup of tea in front of a face whose lower half had been eaten away by the tuberculosis bacterium. Schrödinger tried to conceal his disgust, but was unable to take his eyes off her, gripped by the fear that those deformities, which affected a small proportion of the ill, causing their lymph nodes to swell like clusters of grapes, might one day lay waste to his own features. His unease before the woman affected the entire table; in a matter of seconds, half his fellow diners—men and women as grotesquely disfigured as her—were staring at the physicist as if he were a dog shitting in the aisle of a church. Schrödinger tried to leave, but he felt the graze of a hand on his thigh beneath the white tablecloth. Not an erotic caress, but something akin to an electric shock, it immediately restored his composure. He turned to the owner of the hand, its fingers still resting on his knee like a butterfly with folded wings, and saw Doctor Herwig's daughter. Schrödinger did not dare smile for fear of frightening her; after thanking her with his eyes for the gesture, he drank his coffee intently, trying not to move a muscle, while his newfound calm spread from one table to the next, as though the girl had touched not him but everyone at the same time. When nothing was audible but the soft clinking of plates and silverware, Miss Herwig pulled away her hand. She stood up, smoothed out the folds of her dress, and turned to the door, stopping only to greet two boys, twins, who grabbed her around the neck and would not let go until she had given each a kiss. Schrödinger asked for a second cup of coffee, but could not bring himself to taste it. He remained seated there until everyone had left the room, then walked to reception, asked for a pencil and paper, and left a note for Doctor Herwig declaring his willingness, indeed his eagerness, to help the man's daughter.

To prevent any interruption to Schrödinger's work schedule, Doctor Herwig proposed that the lessons take place in the girl's room, which connected with that of the physicist through a communicating door. The day of the first class, Schrödinger spent the entire morning getting himself ready. He bathed, shaved carefully, felt compelled at first to leave his hair untouched, but then combed it, thinking he should offer a more formal image, not least because, as he well knew, women often admired his high, clear forehead. He enjoyed a light lunch, and at four in the afternoon heard the clicking of the lock on the other side of the door, followed by two barely audible knocks on the wood, which gave him the beginnings of an erection, so that he had to sit down and wait a few moments before entering Miss Herwig's room.

The scent of wood filled Schrödinger's nostrils as soon as he passed through the door, but the oak panelling of the walls was hardly visible beneath the hundreds of beetles, dragonflies, butterflies, crickets, spiders, cockroaches and fireflies pierced with needles or posed inside tiny glass domes with miniature replicas of their natural habitats. In the middle of this immense insectarium, Miss Herwig awaited him, hunched over her desk, looking at him as though he were a new specimen for her collection. In the young woman's imposing presence, Schrödinger felt, for a fraction of a second, like a timid schoolboy before a teacher impatient at his tardiness, and he offered her an extravagant bow at which she could not help but smile. The physicist noticed her small teeth and the slight gap between her incisors, and only then did he see her as she really was: little more than a girl. Ashamed at the fantasies he had incubated from the time of their meeting in the canteen, Schrödinger took a chair, and they set immediately to studying the problems from the entrance examination. The girl's mind was agile, and Schrödinger was surprised how much he enjoyed her company, even as his lust for her seemed to have vanished. They worked for two hours, almost entirely in silence, and when she had finished the last of the exercises, they set an hour for the following day, and the girl offered him a cup of tea. Schrödinger drank while the girl showed him the insects her father had collected, which she herself mounted and preserved. When she suggested she should not waste any more of his time, Schrödinger saw that night had fallen. He took his leave from the doorway with the same genuflection as on arrival, and, despite Miss Herwig's smile, no different from before, Schrödinger returned to his room feeling utterly ridiculous.

Despite his weariness, he was unable to fall asleep. When he closed his eyes, all he could see was Miss Herwig crouched at her desk, wrinkling her nose and wetting her lips with the tip of her tongue. He got up in ill humour and picked up the papers he had thrown to the floor the day before. He tried to put them in order, but even this proved overwhelming. He was incapable of untangling which argument led to which conclusion; all that was clear was the equation on the final page—which seemed to capture perfectly the movement of an electron inside an atom—but there was no evident connection between it and what he had written before. Nothing like this had ever happened to him. How could he have created something that not even he himself could understand? It was madness! He laid the sheets of paper between the worn covers of the notebook and locked it inside a drawer. Unwilling to give up, he worked on an article he had begun six months earlier, in which he analysed a strange acoustic phenomenon he had experienced during the war: after a great explosion, the sound waves weakened as they moved away from their point of origin, but at a certain distance, around fifty kilometres away, they seemed to return even more powerfully than before, as though, in advancing through space, they had moved backwards in time. Schrödinger, who at times could hear even the heartbeats of those around him, was fascinated by the inexplicable rebirth of sound from the verge of extinction, but, despite his best efforts, he could work no more than twenty minutes before his thoughts returned to Miss Herwig. He went back to bed and stuffed himself with sleeping pills. That night, he had two nightmares: in the first, a giant wave broke through the panes of his window and flooded his room to the ceiling; in the second, Schrödinger was floating naked on a choppy sea, just a few metres from the shore. He was exhausted and could hardly keep his nose above the water, but he did not dare swim in, for a beautiful woman was waiting for him on the sands, her skin black as coal, dancing on the corpse of her husband.

His dreams did not prevent his waking up in a good mood, and full of energy; he knew that Miss Herwig would be waiting for him at eleven. When he saw her, he realized she was in no condition to endure a lesson. Pallid, with sunken eyes, she told him she had spent the better part of the night watching a female aphid spawn dozens of tiny offspring. What was marvellous but at the same time horrible about the process, the girl said, was that these offspring would in turn produce offspring of their own after just a few hours of life; these new creatures were themselves gestating while still inside their mother. Three generations were nestled one inside the other, in a sort of dreadful Russian doll, a super-organism that embodied nature's tendency to overabundance, which elsewhere compelled certain birds to produce more chicks than they could feed, so that the dominant fledgling would murder its siblings, pushing them from the nest. In some species, such as the shark, it was even worse, Miss Herwig explained, as the eggs hatched inside the mother's womb, with teeth sufficiently developed to devour the young that came after them; this fratricidal predation gave them the necessary nourishment to survive during the first weeks of life when they were vulnerable enough to be preyed on by the same fish they themselves would feed on as adults. Following her father's instructions, Miss Herwig had divided the members of the three generations of aphids, placing them in jars and exposing them to a pesticide that stained the glass such a striking shade of blue it seemed as though she were looking at the primordial colour of the sky. The insects had died instantly, but she had dreamt that night of their legs covered in blue dust, and had hardly got any rest at all. She would be unable to pay attention to her lessons, she said, but perhaps Herr Schrödinger would be willing to accompany her on a walk around the lake, to see if the cold air restored her strength?

Outside, winter dominated the landscape. The edges of the lake were frozen, and Schrödinger stopped to pick up little slivers of ice that dissolved slowly in the warmth of his hands. When they had reached the lake's furthest edge, Miss Herwig asked what he was working on. Schrödinger spoke to her of Heisenberg's ideas and de Broglie's thesis, and described the apparent epiphany he had had his first night in the clinic and the strange equation it had produced. At first sight, it resembled closely the kind of physics used to calculate wave mechanics in the sea or the dispersion of sound through the atmosphere; but to apply it to the inner functioning of the atom, to the movement of electrons, Schrödinger had needed to include an imaginary number in his formula: the square root of minus one. In practical terms, this meant that a part of the wave his equation described escaped the three dimensions of space. Its crests and troughs travelled through multiple dimensions in a highly abstract realm that could only be described by pure mathematics. Beautiful as they were, Schrödinger's waves were not a part of this world. It was obvious to him that his new equation described electrons as if they were waves. The problem was to understand what the hell was waving! As he spoke, Miss Herwig sat on a wooden bench at the edge of the lake. The physicist sat down next to her, and she opened a book she held in her hands, reading the following passage: "One ghost succeeds the other like waves on the illusory sea of birth and death. In the course of a life, there is nothing but the rise and fall of material and mental forms, while the unfathomable reality remains. In every creature sleeps an infinite intelligence, hidden and unknown, but destined to awaken, to tear the volatile web of the sensory mind, break the chrysalis of flesh, and conquer time and space." Schrödinger recognized those same ideas that had obsessed him for years, and she told him that the winter before, a writer had spent some time in the clinic after having lived for four decades in Japan, where he had converted to Buddhism; it was he who had given her those first lessons in Asian philosophy. Schrödinger and Miss Herwig passed the rest of the afternoon talking of Hinduism, Vedanta and the Great Vehicle of the Mayahana with the enthusiasm of two people discovering, without any prior indication, that they shared a secret. When they saw a flash of light illuminate the mountains in the distance, Miss Herwig said they should return right away to the sanatorium, because a storm was closing in. Schrödinger looked for an excuse to remain with her. It was not the first time he had become obsessed with a woman that young, but there was something different about Miss Herwig, something that disarmed him, that put his self-confidence in jeopardy. When they reached the foot of the stairs, he wondered whether to offer her his arm to lean on, and, in his hesitation, he slipped and sprained his ankle. They had to take him to his room on a stretcher, and he needed her help to remove his shoe from his swollen foot before climbing into bed.

Over the following days, Miss Herwig played the part of nurse and student. She brought him his food and his morning paper and obliged him to take the remedies her father had prescribed him, offering him her shoulder so he could hop to the bathroom. Schrödinger longed for those brief moments of contact and would drink up to three litres of water a day as an excuse to have her close, indifferent to the pain that unnecessary back-and-forth caused him. They continued their lessons in the evenings. The first day she sat in a chair, resting her feet on the bed, but Schrödinger had to strain his neck to see her notebook, and so she wound up sitting beside him, so close he could feel the heat emanating from her body. He could hardly resist the urge to touch her, but he tried to remain completely immobile to prevent her taking fright, even if it seemed this familiarity did not bother her in the least. Schrödinger would masturbate as soon as she had left the room, when he could still close his eyes and see her sitting by his side. Afterwards a tremendous guilt would beset him. Because he could not reach the bathroom without her help, he would clean himself with a cloth he kept hidden beneath the bed, like an adolescent still living at his parents' house. Every time he did it, he promised himself he would speak to Doctor Herwig the next day and cancel their lessons. Then he would call his wife to pick him up and would never set foot in the clinic again, even if it meant coughing himself to death in the streets like a beggar. Anything was better than bearing this infantile infatuation, which deepened the longer they spent together. When she gave him a sumptuous illustrated copy of the Bhagavad Gita, he dared to confess to her a recurring dream that had tortured him since he began to study the Vedas.

In his nightmare, the goddess Kali would sit on his chest like an enormous beetle, crushing him so that he could not move. With her necklace of human heads, and brandishing swords, axes and knives in her many arms, she would bathe him in drops of blood that fell from the tip of her tongue and jets of milk from her swollen breasts, rubbing his groin until he was no longer capable of bearing the arousal, at which point she would decapitate him and swallow his genitals. Miss Herwig listened to him impassively and told him his dream was not a nightmare, but a blessing: of all the forms taken on by the female aspect of the divine, Kali was the most compassionate, because she granted *moksha*— liberation—to her children, and her love for them extended beyond all human comprehension. Her black skin, she said, was the symbol of the void that transcends all form, the cosmic uterus in which all phenomena gestated, while her necklace of skulls comprised the egos she had freed from the principal object of their identification, which was nothing less than the body itself. The castration Schrödinger suffered at the Dark Mother's hands was the greatest gift he could receive, a mutilation necessary so that his new consciousness could be born.

Confined to his bed for hours with no means of distraction, Schrödinger made great advances with his equation. Its power and scope became increasingly evident the more he approached a final version of it, though its significance in physical terms seemed to him ever more strange and indecipherable. According to his calculations, the electron was diffuse around the nucleus, like a cloud, and it oscillated like a wave trapped between the walls of a pool. But was that wave a real phenomenon or merely a trick that allowed one to calculate the particle's location from one moment to the next? Harder yet to understand was the fact that his equation showed not a single wave for each electron, but an extraordinary variety of them, superimposed. Did all describe the same object, or did each represent a possible world? Schrödinger considered the second possibility: those multiple waves would be the first glimpse of something completely new, each a brief flash of a universe that was born when the electron leapt from one state to the other, branching out to populate the infinite, like the jewels of Indra's net. But such a thing was inconceivable. Rack his brain as he might, he could not understand how he had strayed so far from his original intent. He had hoped to simplify the atomic world, had looked for a common attribute to all things, and had given birth to a greater mystery. His malaise kept him from working further, and he could think of nothing but the pain in his ankle and the body of Miss Herwig, who had missed her lessons over the past few days to help her father organize the Christmas celebrations.

On Christmas Eve, all the patients at the clinic—irrespective of the severity of their illness—attended a party that had become increasingly elaborate as the years went by. The celebration incorporated traditions from all over Europe and even beyond the Levant, pagan rites that had been lost with time and that celebrated not the coming of Christ, but the winter solstice, the return of the light after December 21, the longest and darkest night of the year in the northern hemisphere. The patients' inflexible routine was broken, and, just as during the Roman Saturnalia, they walked half-nude through the halls, blowing whistles, beating drums and shaking bells before choosing their disguises and coming together for a great banquet. Schrödinger hated the celebration, and the first thing he did when Miss Herwig came to his room to resume her lessons was complain that the hellish racket of that carnival of imbeciles would keep him from sleeping all night. To the physicist's astonishment, she took off her earrings, placed them in her mouth, and pulled the pearls away from the clasp with her teeth; after drying them on the cuffs of her dress, she bent over and put them in his ears. She explained that she did this when she had a migraine, and insisted that he keep them as a token of gratitude for the time he had devoted to her. Schrödinger asked her if she would take part in the festivities that year, imagining her naked and masked, though he knew that she never did so. She confessed that she hated Christmas; it was the period of highest mortality in the clinic, and neither drunken revelry nor frenetic dancing cleared her mind of so much death. Schrödinger was about to reply, but she fell backwards over the bed as if a bullet had struck her in the centre of her chest. "Do you know the first thing I'll do when I get out of here?" she asked him with a smile crossing her face. "I'll get drunk, and I'll sleep with the ugliest man I can find." "Why the ugliest?" Schrödinger asked, removing the pearls from his ears. "Because I want my first time to be for me and me alone," she said, turning her neck to look him in the eyes. Schrödinger asked her if she had ever been with a man. "No man, no woman, no animal, no bird, no beast, no god, no demon; no material or incorporeal being, not this, not that, not the other," Miss Herwig recited, rising slowly in the bed, like a corpse returning briefly to the world of the living. Schrödinger could hold back no more: he told her she was the most fascinating creature he had ever met, and that she had mesmerized him from the moment she had touched him in the canteen. The little time they had spent together had been the greatest happiness he had known over the past ten years, and the mere thought of her filled him with zeal. The idea of returning to Zurich terrified him, as he was certain she would pass her entrance exams and leave for boarding school and he would never be able to see her again. Miss Herwig barely moved while he spoke, and stared intently at the window; on the other side of the glass, an endless row of tiny lights rose up the path snaking up from the valley to the summit of the Weisshorn, thousands of torches shining brighter as the procession advanced and the sun vanished beneath the horizon. "When I was a girl, I had an uncontrollable fear of the dark," she finally told him. "I would spend the whole night awake, reading by the light of candles my grandfather had given me, and I couldn't sleep till the sun had begun to rise. I was so fragile in those days, my father didn't dare punish me; his solution was to tell me that light was a finite resource. If too much of it were used, it would vanish, and darkness would reign over all things. That fear of an endless night convinced me to snuff out my candles, but I adopted the even stranger custom of going to bed before night fell. In summer that wasn't difficult, the sun would go down late and I could take advantage of the entire day, but in wintertime, I had to go to bed not long after lunch, and I spent more time asleep than awake. The worst night of the year was this one, the winter solstice. The few children in the clinic would go on playing till midnight, dancing and running through the hallways, while I had to wait until the morning after to gather up the sweets that had been lost in the darkness and weave wreaths from the stomped tinsel of the decorations. I was nine when I decided to confront my fear. In this same room, in front of this same window, I stood while the sun sank behind the horizon, so quickly that it seemed dragged by a force stronger than mere gravity, as if, weary of its own brilliance, it wished to extinguish itself once and for all. I was about to climb under the sheets to cry when I saw the torches on the path. I thought they were my imagination, because in those days I often confused my dreams with reality, but as the lights came closer I could see the silhouettes of those carrying them. When they set alight a gigantic wooden effigy, I saw the men and women dancing around it; opening the window, I heard their songs, carried over with absolute clarity by the mountain air. I dressed as quickly as I could and asked my father to take me up to the burning pyre. He was astonished to see me awake at night, and put everything aside to accompany me. We walked together, holding hands, my palm sweating against his despite the cold, and we returned there year after year, irrespective of the weather or the state of my health, as if it were a covenant we had to rekindle again and again. This is the first night when we won't go. There's no longer any need; that same fire is now alight inside me and is consuming all that I have ever been. I no longer feel things as I did before. No ties bind me to others, I treasure no memories, no desires drive me onwards. My father, the sanatorium, this country, the mountain, the wind, the words that come from my mouth, all seem to me things as distant as the dreams of a woman long dead. This body you see eats, grows, walks, talks and smiles, but there is nothing left inside it but ashes. I have lost my fear of the night, Herr Schrödinger, and you should do the same." Miss Herwig stood and walked to her room. She stopped an instant at the threshold, leant the weight of her body against the frame, and it seemed as though she were about to lose her strength. Schrödinger asked her not to leave, and tried to stand to reach her, but before he could take a step she had closed the door behind her.

Schrödinger spent the rest of the night with her pearls in his ears, incapable of banishing the image of the young woman bringing them to her mouth, her tensed lips biting the clasp, the glimmer of her spittle as she removed them. Humiliated by his confession and in despair at his inability to sleep, he took them out and masturbated, holding them in the palm of his hand. When he ejaculated, he heard Miss Herwig suffer an attack of coughing that seemed as if it would never end, and he hobbled to the basin, disgusted with himself. He soaked the pearls over and over, letting the water restore their gleam before putting them back in his ears, not to muffle the revelry, but to deaden the interminable hacking of his neighbour, which he heard all night, not knowing whether its pitiable staccato was emerging from the throat of the woman he loved or his imagination, for when he awoke the next morning, he still heard it, regular and maddening as a dripping tap, and it seemed to have invaded his own body, and he could not move without coughing himself breathless.

He gave himself over to the routines of the ill.

He floated around the swimming pools, slept out in the open beneath a layer of animal pelts, and burned his lungs with the glacial air of the mountains and the searing heat of the saunas; he let his back be massaged with oils, his body tortured with cupping glasses, dragging himself from room to room with the rest of the inmates, enjoying the consolation of a person whose entire life has been reduced to the inflexible repetition of therapy. The only real benefit he noticed from all of this was an almost miraculous recovery in his ankle. Soon he could walk without need of a cane, which permitted him to spend as little time as possible in his room; a considerable relief, as from there he could hear the sobs and groans of his neighbour as clearly as if they were sharing a bed. He spent his nights with a girl who worked as a lifeguard at the clinic's pool and slept with Schrödinger and his fellow patients in exchange for money—an arrangement which Doctor Herwig tolerated. During the day, when he had no treatments, Schrödinger would stroll through the clinic like a sleepwalker, crossing the endless hallways and trying not to think of Miss Herwig, his equation or his wife, who would certainly have spent the previous weeks fucking incessantly while he was fantasizing about an adolescent. He thought of the classes he would have to resume as soon as he had recovered, of the tedium of repetition, the blank stares of his students and the texture of chalk as it crumbled between his fingers, and suddenly he seemed to see his entire future life as though it were composed of parallel and simultaneous scenes opening like a fan and leading off in all possible directions; in one, he and Miss Herwig ran away to start their lives together; in another, his health took a sudden turn and he died there in the clinic, drowning in his own blood; in a third, his wife left him, but he flourished, professionally; in most of these scenarios, Schrödinger continued down the same path he had taken up until then, remaining married to Anny and working as a professor until death overtook him at some unknown European university. Laid low by depression, he walked down to the first floor and out onto the terrace to take some fresh air. He was unready for the desolation he would see outside. It seemed as though someone had erased the entire world. Where the lake had once been, surrounded by trees and cradled by the distant profile of the mountains, there was now only an immense burial shroud, a layer of snow so even and dense that it obscured every last detail of the landscape. All the roads would be blocked. Schrödinger could not leave the clinic even if he wished. He went back inside with a sensation of seclusion, of claustrophobia, that he could hardly bear.

His health worsened as the new year approached. When he was overcome with fever, he had to give up his walks and submit to bed rest. His skin felt raw, and even the touch of his sheets bothered him. If he closed his eyes, he could hear the clicking of the spoons in the canteen, the movement of the chess pieces in the recreation room, the shriek of the steam in the laundry. Rather than ignore them, he concentrated on them, trying to drown out the sound of Miss Herwig's breath, that thin thread of air that could barely enter through her swollen throat and was incapable of filling her lungs. Schrödinger had to restrain his desire to break down the door between them and hold the sick girl in his arms; at the same time, he could not even gather the energy to put a title to the article in which he had formalized his equation. He had decided to publish it as it was and let others unravel its significance, if there was any. Truthfully, it no longer mattered to him: every time Miss Herwig coughed, he was shaken by uncontrollable spasms. This same relapse seemed to have affected everyone at the sanatorium. The cleaning staff had not come to his room in two days, and when he called reception to complain, they told him everyone was busy with more urgent cases than his own. That same morning, two boys had died: the twins Schrödinger had seen in the dining room hanging on Miss Herwig's neck. Schrödinger could give no expression to his rage, and simply asked them to advise him when the roads were once again clear. He wanted to leave as soon as possible.

The next day there was a blizzard. Schrödinger spent the entire morning in bed, watching how the snowflakes accumulated on his window ledge until at last he fell back to sleep. Two knocks on his door woke him. He got up, his hair in disarray, food stains on his pyjamas, but the man he saw when he opened the door looked infinitely worse; Doctor Herwig resembled one of those soldiers Schrödinger had seen return from the trenches, eyes filmy from clouds of chlorine gas. His host begged his pardon for the pitiful state of Schrödinger's room. The clinic was going through a crisis. At reception, he had been told Schrödinger was planning to depart, and he had come to convey a message from his daughter: might a final lesson be possible before he left? The doctor looked at the ground as he spoke, as though he were asking for something unpardonable. Schrödinger could hardly conceal his enthusiasm. While the doctor went on to say that he didn't wish to trouble him and that he understood perfectly if the request was out of line, Schrödinger dressed clumsily, explaining he was not inconvenienced in the least, quite the contrary, it would be a pleasure, he could do it right then, right away, he just needed five minutes to comb his hair, or not even that, if he could just find his goddamned shoes, where the hell had he left them! The doctor watched him stomping from one end of the room to the other with the bewildered expression of a man who has lost what matters most to him in the world—an expression Schrödinger could not fathom until he saw Miss Herwig's state.

Pale and skeletal, she was submerged in piles of cushions that closed in on her like the petals of a monstrous flower. She was so thin that Schrödinger began to wonder whether time had passed differently for each of them: it was impossible that a human being should undergo a change so drastic in a matter of days. The skin on her neck had turned transparent and the veins were so clearly marked that Schrödinger could have measured her pulse just by looking at her. Sweat pearled on her forehead, her hands shook from fever, and her body seemed to have shrunk to that of a nine-year-old girl. Schrödinger did not dare enter the room. He stayed standing there in the doorway, with Doctor Herwig waiting behind him, until she opened her eyes, looking at him with the same expression of reproach that had greeted him during their first lesson. The girl asked her father to leave the two of them alone, and told Schrödinger to sit down.

Schrödinger walked towards a chair, but she patted the mattress beside her, inviting him over to the bed. Schrödinger did not know where to look: he could not reconcile the image of the woman he had dreamt of with the one he now saw. He felt immense relief when she asked him to examine her notebook; she had completed her final test. Schrödinger looked at the exercises, and, at first, the numbers seemed to him unintelligible; he was so shaken that he could not solve the basic equations he himself had devised for her. Playing for time, he asked her to explain to him how she had arrived at a certain result, the only one that evinced a certain degree of difficulty. Miss Herwig told him she could not: her mind had presented her with the results, and she had had to work backwards to write out her calculations. Schrödinger confessed to a similar affliction, but said he had abandoned that intuitive approach to mathematics when he entered the university, in order to satisfy his professors. Only now had he begun to give his intuition free rein, and he had gone so far he had no idea how to find the way back. Miss Herwig asked him if he had made progress on his equation. Schrödinger stood up and began pacing from side to side while he spoke of the strangest aspect of his formula.

In appearance, he said, it was very simple: applied to any physical system, it allowed one to describe its future evolution. If used for a particle, such as an electron, it revealed all its possible states. The problem lay in its central term—the soul of the equation—which Schrödinger had represented with the Greek letter ψ and had baptized as the "wave function". All the information one could wish to have about a quantum system was contained in the wave function. But Schrödinger did not know what it was. It had the form of a wave, but could not be a real physical phenomenon, because it moved outside this world, in multidimensional space. Perhaps it was only a mathematical chimera. The only certain thing was its power, which seemed unlimited. In theory, Schrödinger could apply his equation to the entire universe: the result would be a wave function that would encapsulate the future evolution of all things. But how would he convince others that such a thing could exist? ψ was undetectable: it would leave no trace on any type of instrument. Neither the most advanced apparatus nor the most ingenious experiments could capture it. It was something new, of a nature totally distinct from that of the world it described with unsettling precision. Schrödinger knew it was the discovery he had longed for his entire life, but he had no way of defending it. He had not derived his equation from pre-existing principles. His thinking had not departed from any known basis. The equation itself was a principle, and his mind had pulled it from nothing. When he turned to see whether Miss Herwig had been able to follow his long disquisition, he found her sound asleep.

For Schrödinger, she was no less beautiful than ever. He pushed aside the cushions surrounding her to pull back a lock of hair that had covered her face, and he could not resist touching her further. He caressed her neck, her shoulders, her collarbones, followed the strap of her nightgown to the soft curvature of her breasts and circled the place where he imagined her nipples lay. He continued on towards her navel and stopped a few millimetres from her pubis, too timid to go further. He closed his eyes and held his breath, listening to Miss Herwig's clipped respiration, and when he opened them, she threw off the sheet that covered her and he saw her transformed into the goddess of his dreams, a black-skinned corpse covered in suppurating wounds and scabs, her tongue lolling from her smiling skull while her hands pulled open the shrivelled lips of her vagina, where the legs of a massive beetle flailed, trapped in a tangle of snow-white hairs. The vision lasted a fraction of a second, then the sheet once more covered Miss Herwig, who was sleeping as though she had never awakened. Still, Schrödinger ran out in dread. He gathered his papers and fled the centre without paying his bill, dragging his suitcases against the stormy wind and trying to reach the train station, not knowing if the roads would be closed from the snow.

IV.
The Kingdom of Uncertainty

In Zurich, Schrödinger not only recovered his health but gave the impression of a man possessed by genius.

He built on his equation until it comprised a complete mechanics developed over five articles written in only six months, each of them more brilliant than its predecessor. Max Planck, who had been the first to postulate the existence of energy quanta, wrote to tell him he had read them "with the pleasure of a child hearing the solution to a riddle that has troubled him for years". Paul Dirac went even further: the eccentric English genius, whose mathematical abilities were legendary, said that the Austrian's equation contained practically all physics known up to that moment and—at least in principle—all of chemistry as well. Schrödinger had touched glory.

No one dared deny the importance of this new wave mechanics, but pretty soon some began to ask themselves the same questions that had troubled Schrödinger in the Villa Herwig. "It is a truly beautiful theory. One of the most perfect, precise and elegant man has discovered. But there is something strange in it. It's as if it were warning us: don't take me seriously. The world I reveal is not the one you are thinking of when you employ me," wrote Robert Oppenheimer, one of the first to question what wave functions actually had to say about reality. Schrödinger devoted himself to travelling through Europe expounding his ideas, and applause met him wherever he went, until he came across Werner Heisenberg.

In the Munich auditorium, the Austrian was unable to finish his presentation before his young rival leapt to the stage and began erasing his calculations from the blackboard, replacing them with his horrible matrices. For Heisenberg, what Schrödinger proposed was an indefensible step backward. Methods from classical physics could not be used to explain the quantum world. Atoms were not simply marbles! Electrons were not water droplets! Schrödinger's equation might be exquisite and even useful, but it erred in what was most essential when it ignored the radical strangeness of matter at the smallest scale. What enraged Heisenberg was not the wave function—though who the hell knew what that thing was?—but a matter of principles: however much the Austrian's contrivance had bewitched all who encountered it, he knew it was a dead end, a blind alley leading them away from true comprehension. Because none of them would dare to do what he had achieved in the midst of his torments in Heligoland: not merely to calculate but to think in a quantum manner. Heisenberg shouted louder, trying and failing to make himself heard over the public's scorn, while Schrödinger remained perfectly calm; for the first time in his life, he felt in complete control of his faculties. Convinced of the undeniable value of his work, he was unmoved by the young German's tantrum. Before the host of the event threw Heisenberg out on his ear, egged on by all those present, Schrödinger told him there surely existed things in the world which were immune to analysis through common sense metaphors—but the internal structure of the atom was not one of them.

Heisenberg returned home broken, but unwilling to accept defeat. For two years, he attacked Schrödinger's ideas in publications and seminars of all sorts, but fate seemed to smile on his opponent; in what seemed to be the coup de grâce in their quarrel, Schrödinger published an article showing that his procedure and Heisenberg's were mathematically equivalent. Applied to a problem, they gave the exact same results. They were merely two ways of approaching an object, but his had the immense advantage of being intuitively comprehensible. There was no need to tear out one's eyes to look at subatomic particles, as young Heisenberg liked to say: all you had to do was close them and imagine. "When discussing subatomic theories," Schrödinger wrote at the end of his article, "we may perfectly well speak in the singular."

Heisenberg's matrix mechanics was doomed to oblivion. His epiphany in Heligoland would be nothing more than a postscript in the annals of science. With every day that passed, it seemed, someone published a new piece of work presenting results obtained with his matrices, but translated into the elegant wave language of Schrödinger. Heisenberg's contempt reached fever pitch when he found himself incapable of deriving the spectrum of a hydrogen atom with his own theory and was forced to rely on his rival's equations: he performed his calculus gnashing his teeth, as if trying to crack them one by one.

Even though he was still a very young man, his parents pestered him continually to stop wasting his talent and seek out a position as a full-blown professor in Germany. Heisenberg had travelled to Denmark, where he worked as an assistant to Niels Bohr, living in a tiny attic of the Bohr Institute for Theoretical Physics at the University of Copenhagen, beneath a sloping roof that forced him to move about with his head bowed, reminding him daily of what his father called his "subservience" to the Danish physicist.

Bohr and Heisenberg had a great deal in common: like his pupil, the Dane was famous for the almost deliberate obscurity of his arguments, and, though everyone respected him, many said that his ideas tended to stray closer to philosophy than to physics. Bohr was one of the first to accept Heisenberg's new postulates, but he also proved a source of eternal frustration to his student, being inclined to tolerate both Schrödinger's waves and Heisenberg's matrices, unified through a principle he referred to as complementarity.

Rather than working to resolve the contradictions between the two approaches, Bohr embraced them. In his view, the attributes of elementary particles were only valid in a given context and arose from a relationship. No single frame of reference could encompass them. Measured in experiments of one type, they would exhibit the properties of a wave; in another, they would appear to be particles. These perspectives were mutually exclusive, antagonistic, and at the same time complementary: neither was a perfect reflection, and both were models of the world. Combined, they gave a more perfect notion of nature. Heisenberg detested complementarity. He was certain they needed to develop a single conceptual system, not two contradictory ones. And he was ready to do anything to achieve this: if the price of understanding quantum mechanics was upsetting our very concept of reality, he, for one, was willing to pay it.

When he was not shut up in his room working, pacing from one end to the other with his head down and his shoulders hunched, he would argue with Bohr until dawn. Their dispute lasted for months and turned increasingly violent. When Heisenberg lost his voice screaming at Bohr, the Dane brought forward his winter vacation to take a break from his irritable pupil, whose stubbornness was only rivalled by his own, and whose character he had come to loathe. Without Bohr to provoke him, Heisenberg was left alone with his demons, and soon he had become his own worst enemy. He broke off into two people, giving long monologues that argued for his position and then Bohr's, and his enthusiasm was such that he could soon imitate perfectly the insufferable pedantry of his teacher, as if he had developed a split personality. Betraying his own intuitions, he set aside his columns of numbers and matrices and tried to imagine the electron as a bundle of waves. What did Schrödinger's equation actually describe when applied to an electron revolving around a nucleus? It was not a wave proper, that much was clear on account of its dimensionality. Perhaps it showed all the states the electron could inhabit— its energy levels, velocities and coordinates—but like hazy snapshots, superimposed, one atop the other. Some were in focus: these were the most probable states for the electron. Or was it a wave of probabilities? A statistical distribution? The French had translated the wave function as *densité de probabilité de présence*. That was all Schrödinger's mechanics revealed: blurry images, a ghostly presence, diffuse and undefined. The vague outline of something not of this world. But what would happen if one considered that point of view and Heisenberg's own at the same time? The result was absurd and intriguing: an electron that was both a particle confined to a given point and a wave extending through time and space. Overcome by all these paradoxes and seething at his incapacity to banish Schrödinger's ideas, he left to walk through the park surrounding the university.

He did not notice the passing hours until midnight, when the cold obliged him to take refuge in the only place still open at that time, a bar where Copenhagen's bohemians gathered, and artists, poets, criminals and prostitutes bought their doses of cocaine and hashish. Heisenberg's sobriety bordered on the puritanical, and though he passed by there every day, and many of his colleagues were regulars, he had never entered before. The stench when he opened the door struck him like a blow to the face. Had it not been for the cold, he would have returned to his quarters. He headed to the back and sat at the only empty table. He raised a hand to call over a man dressed in black who he assumed to be a waiter, but instead of taking his order, the man sat at the other end of the table and looked at him with burning eyes. "What can I offer you tonight, Professor?" he said, removing a tiny bottle from the interior of his jacket. He looked back, positioning himself so the owner of the bar would not see Heisenberg's attempts to get his attention. "Don't worry about him, Professor, everyone is welcome here, even people like you," he said, winking at him and placing the bottle on the table. Heisenberg felt immediate contempt for the stranger. Why did this man at least ten years his senior insist on addressing him so formally? Heisenberg continued trying to summon the barman, but the shoulders of the stranger, slumped over the table like a giant drunken bear, blocked his view almost entirely. "You won't believe me when I say this, Professor, but not long ago a seven-year-old child was sitting in the same chair you are in now, crying nonstop. The saddest child in the world, I promise you, I can still hear him sobbing. And who can concentrate on their writing with such a racket? Have you tried hashish, sir? No, of course you haven't. Today, no one has time for eternity. Only children, children and drunks, not serious people like you, Professor, those on the verge of changing the world. Or am I wrong?" Heisenberg did not answer. He had decided he would not play along, and was about to stand when he saw something metallic flash in the man's hand. "There's no hurry, Professor, we have the entire night before us. Relax, let me buy you a drink. Though, truth be told, I'd say you could use something stronger, no?" He spilled the contents of the bottle into what was left of his beer and pushed the glass towards Heisenberg. "You look tired, Professor. You should take better care of yourself. Did you know the first symptom of a psychological disturbance is the inability to contend with the future? If you consider that, you will realize how implausible it is that we are able to exert control over even an hour of our lives. How hard it is to control our thoughts! You, for example—it is obvious you are possessed. That you are in thrall to your intellect as a degenerate is in thrall to a woman's cunt. You are bewitched, Professor, you've been sucked inside your own head. Come on, drink. Don't make me ask you twice." The physicist pushed himself away, but the stranger grabbed his shoulder and brought the glass to Heisenberg's lips. Panicked, he looked around to ask for help and saw that the entire bar was staring at him impassively, as though present at a ritual each of them had been obliged to undergo. He opened his mouth and drank the green liquid in a single swig. The man smiled, leant back in his seat, and laced his fingers together behind his head. "Now, Professor, you and I can talk like two civilized people. Believe me, I know about these things. We must let space and time be woven together like a single fibre, we must always remain in motion. Who could bear to stay in a single place his whole life? That's fine for a stone, but not for a man like yourself, Professor. Have you listened to the wireless recently? I have a programme that might interest you. It's conceived for children, but curious children, brave children like yourself. I tell them about all the great catastrophes of our era. The tragedies, the massacres, the horrors. Did you know five hundred people died in a flood in Mississippi last month? The water flowed with such force that the levees broke and the people drowned in their sleep. There are those who think children shouldn't know these things, but that doesn't worry me. The horrible thing isn't the bodies floating in the water, their swollen flesh falling off their bones. No. The truly grotesque thing is that I found out about all of this almost instantaneously. From the other side of the planet, word reached me that my adored Uncle Willy, that old bastard, and my beloved Aunt Clara, the old bitch, had saved themselves from the water by climbing up on the roof of their candy store. Candy! If that isn't black magic, you tell me what is. It doesn't matter how many people have died or how many have been saved, Professor—today, all of us are victims. You are too intelligent not to realize that. I still remember the first time I received a telephone call. I was in my grandfather's house and my mother called me from the hotel where she liked to spend the holidays to get away from me. As soon as I heard the ring, I picked up the receiver and pressed my head against the speaker, giving myself over to the voice emerging from it, and there was nothing that could mitigate that violence. Impotent, I suffered as I saw how my consciousness of time was destroyed, my resolve, my sense of duty and proportion! And to whom do we owe this magnificent inferno if not to you, to people like you? Tell me, Professor, when did all this madness begin? When did we cease to understand the world?" The man held his face in his hands, stretching his skin out to both sides until he was utterly deformed, and then let himself collapse over the table, as though no longer capable of supporting his prodigious weight. Heisenberg used this moment to escape.

He ran without knowing where to, lost in the fog with his arms outstretched in front of him, groping at the air like a blind man. When his legs cramped, he collapsed on top of the roots of a gigantic oak and felt as if his heart would explode. He had made his way far into the park and could no longer see the light of the street lamps. What had that bastard drugged him with? He was shivering from the cold, his tongue was dry, his vision blurred, adrenalin was rushing through his body, and he could barely contain his longing to weep. All he wanted was to return to his attic, but he was too nauseated to stand. When he tried, the landscape began to spin around him, so quickly he had to hug the tree trunk and close his eyes.

When he opened them, tiny orbs of light floated in the air around him, glimmering like a parade of fireflies. He no longer felt the cold, his legs no longer shivered. He was lucid and disoriented at the same time, just as if he had awakened from a dream. The forest was now unrecognizable; the roots were throbbing like veins, the branches swayed even though he could not feel the wind, and the earth seemed to breathe beneath his feet, but still he was unafraid. A feeling of great peace had come over him, and Heisenberg found it so unusual, given the circumstances, that he feared his tranquillity might turn to panic at any moment. To avoid this, he devoted himself to observing the play of the lights, which covered the entirety of space, falling from treetops or blossoming amid the leaves covering the ground. Most of them disappeared immediately, but some lasted long enough to leave a small trail. With his pupils dilated, Heisenberg noticed that these traces were not continuous lines, but a series of individual points that seemed to be leaping from place to place instantaneously, without passing through the intermediate space. Hypnotized by these hallucinations, he sensed his mind merging with the things he observed: every point of these traces appeared without cause, and the complete trajectory existed in his mind alone, which wove the distinct instances together. Heisenberg concentrated on one of them, but the more he tried to fix it, the more diffuse it became. He dragged himself over the ground on all fours, trying to catch one of the sparks in his hand, laughing like a child chasing after a butterfly, and had nearly caught one when he saw he had been surrounded by a legion of shadows.

Countless men and women with slanted eyes, their bodies sculpted of soot and ash, were stretching out their arms to try and touch him. They thronged around him without managing to advance, humming like a cluster of bees caught in the threads of an invisible web. Heisenberg tried to take the hand of a baby that had broken through the net and was crawling towards him, but an explosion pulverized the figures and brought him to his knees, rummaging in the dirt to try and salvage some trace, some vestige of those phantoms. All he could find was one of the minuscule lights, the single one that had survived. He picked it up with infinite care, hugged it to his chest, and took the path home, fighting against a gale that blew his hair into his eyes and whipped the folds of his jacket, convinced he must do anything to prevent it from going out. He found the exit of the park and headed towards the university building. When he saw the window of his room, he felt something huge looming at his back. He looked over his shoulder and saw a black spectre that darkened everything behind him. He ran in dread, tripped over the cobblestones, and realized it was his own shadow chasing him, cast backward by the light he was holding in his hands. He turned to face his ghost, reached out his arms, and opened his palms. The light and shadow were extinguished in unison.

When Bohr returned from his holiday, Heisenberg told him there was an absolute limit to what we could know about the world.

No sooner had his superior entered the door of the university than Heisenberg grabbed his elbow and led him back out into the park, giving him time neither to leave his baggage nor shake the snow from his overcoat. Combining his own ideas with those of Schrödinger—Heisenberg told Bohr as he dragged his suitcases between the trees, ignoring all his mentor's complaints—he had realized that quantum objects had no fixed identity, but instead dwelt in a space of possibilities. An electron, Heisenberg explained, did not exist in a single place, but in many, and had not one velocity, but several. The wave function showed all those possibilities superimposed. Heisenberg had forgotten the entire accursed debate about particles and waves, and had once more clung to numbers to find his path. Analysing Schrödinger's mathematics and his own, he had discovered that certain properties of a quantum object, such as its position and quantity of motion, were coupled, and the relationship between them evinced strange properties. The more precisely the one was identified, the more uncertain the other became. If, for example, the exact location of an electron was established with certainty, arresting that particle in its orbit like an insect impaled on a pin, then its velocity became utterly undefined; it might be immobile or moving at the speed of light, and there was no way of knowing which. The opposite was true as well. If the electron was endowed with a set quantity of motion, its position was so indeterminate that it might be in the palm of your hand or at the other end of the universe. These two variables were mathematically complementary: establishing the one dissolved the other.

Heisenberg paused to catch his breath. He had been speaking frantically, without stopping, and was soaked with sweat from the effort of lugging Bohr's suitcases through the snow. He had been so lost in his own head that he had not noticed Bohr was now several metres behind him, looking at the ground in extreme concentration. Heisenberg could almost hear the clicking of the gears in his master's mind, which could grind ideas down until he had extracted their marrow; when he approached, Bohr asked if these paired properties were limited to the two variables mentioned, and Heisenberg, panting, said no: they reigned over many aspects of quantum reality, such as the time an electron remained in a state and the energy it possessed in that state. Bohr asked if these relations existed at all levels of matter, or only in the subatomic realm; Heisenberg assured him that they were as true for an electron as for the two of them, but the effects on macroscopic objects were imperceptible, while for a single particle they were vast.

Heisenberg took out the paper on which he had worked out the mathematics behind his new idea, and Bohr sat in the snow to read it. He was silent as he checked the calculations for what seemed to Heisenberg like an eternity, and when he finished, he asked for help getting up. They started walking again to shake off the cold. Bohr asked if this might constitute an experimental limitation, something future generations with advanced technology might overcome. Heisenberg said no: it was something constitutive of matter itself, a principle that governed the way in which all things were created, and that seemed to exclude the possibility that a given phenomenon should possess certain perfectly defined attributes simultaneously. His original intuition had been correct: it was impossible to "see" a quantum entity for the simple reason that *it did not have* a single identity. Illuminating one of its properties necessarily obscured the other. The best description of a quantum system was neither an image nor a metaphor, but rather a set of numbers.

They left the park and plunged into the city streets while they discussed the consequences of Heisenberg's discovery, which Bohr saw as the cornerstone upon which a truly new physics could be founded. In philosophical terms, he told him as he took his arm, this was the end of determinism. Heisenberg's uncertainty principle shredded the hopes of all those who had put their faith in the clockwork universe Newtonian physics had promised. According to the determinists, if one could reveal the laws that governed matter, one could reach back to the most archaic past and predict the most distant future. If everything that occurred was the direct consequence of a prior state, then merely by looking at the present and running the equations it would be possible to achieve a godlike knowledge of the universe. Those hopes were shattered in light of Heisenberg's discovery: what was beyond our grasp was neither the future nor the past, but the present itself. Not even the state of one miserable particle could be perfectly apprehended. However much we scrutinized the fundamentals, there would always be something vague, undetermined, uncertain, as if reality allowed us to perceive the world with crystalline clarity with one eye at a time, but never with both.

Drunk with enthusiasm, Heisenberg noticed that his route through the park was nearly the perfect converse of the one he had traced out the night of his epiphany. He told Bohr this, and the Dane immediately related it to what they were discussing: if we cannot know, at the same time, such basic things as where an electron is and how it moves, we also cannot predict the exact path it will follow between two points, only its multiple possible paths. That was the ingenious thing about Schrödinger's equation: somehow it managed to thread together the infinite destinies of a particle, all its states, all its trajectories, in a single schema—the wave function—showing them all superimposed. A particle could cross space in many ways, but from among them it chose only one. How? Through pure chance. For Heisenberg, it was no longer possible to speak of any subatomic phenomenon with absolute certainty. Where before there had been a cause for every effect, now there was a spectrum of probabilities. In the deepest substrate of all things, physics had not found the solid, unassailable reality Schrödinger and Einstein had dreamt of, ruled over by a rational God pulling the threads of the world, but a domain of wonders and rarities, borne of the whims of a many-armed goddess toying with chance.

When they passed in front of the bar Heisenberg had escaped from, Bohr said all those things were deserving of a beer. The owner had just opened and the place was empty, but the suggestion turned Heisenberg's stomach. He proposed a coffee instead, and perhaps something warm to eat. You don't celebrate with coffee, the Dane replied, and pushed him in.

They sat at the same table Heisenberg had occupied that strange night. Bohr ordered two beers, which they sipped slowly, then two more that they drank down in one go. During the third, Heisenberg confessed all that had happened there: he spoke of the stranger who had drugged him, his fear, the bottle on the table, the man's bearish hands and the glimmer of his knife blade; he described the bitterness of the green liquid, the stranger's irrepressible outburst of emotion and his cowardly escape; he talked of the cold outside, the beauty of his hallucinations, the throbbing roots of the trees, the dance of the fireflies, the tiny ember of light he had caught in his hands and the giant shadow that had followed him to the university. He spoke of all that, and of his life in the weeks afterwards, the storm of ideas unleashed in his head and the unrestrained enthusiasm that had gripped him since that night; but for a strange reason he could explain neither to himself nor to Bohr, for it was one he would not understand until decades later, he was incapable of confessing his vision of the dead baby at his feet, or the thousands of figures who had surrounded him in the forest, as if wishing to warn him of something, before they were carbonized in an instant by that flash of blind light.

V.

God and Dice

On the morning of Monday, October 24, 1927, beneath the grey sky of Brussels, twenty-nine physicists crossed the frost-caked lawn of Leopold Park and entered one of the lecture halls of the Physiology Institute, unaware that five days later they would shake the very foundations of science.

The institute had been built by the industrialist Ernest Solvay for the purpose of demonstrating, insofar as possible, that "the phenomenon of life should be explained by the physical laws that govern the universe, which we may know through observation and the objective study of the facts of the world." Old masters and young revolutionaries had travelled from all over Europe to participate in the Fifth Solvay Conference, the most prestigious scientific gathering of the era. Never before or again were so many geniuses united beneath the same roof: seventeen of them had won, or would go on to win, the Nobel Prize, including Paul Dirac, Wolfgang Pauli, Max Planck and Marie Curie, who had won it twice and was overseeing the conference committee along with Hendrik Lorentz and Albert Einstein.

Although the theme of the conference was "Electrons and Photons", all present knew the true purpose was to analyse quantum mechanics, which was casting doubt on the whole edifice upholding physics.

During the first day, all present spoke. All save Einstein.

On the morning of the second day, Louis de Broglie revealed his new theory of "pilot waves" that explained the movement of the electron as though it were travelling on the crest of a wave like a surfer. He was attacked pitilessly by Schrödinger as well as by the Copenhagen physicists. Unable to defend himself, de Broglie looked to Einstein, who maintained his silence. The timid prince would not open his mouth again for the rest of his time there.

On the third day, two accounts of quantum mechanics faced off.

Full of confidence, Schrödinger defended his waves. He explained that they described perfectly the behaviour of an electron, even if, admittedly, six dimensions were required to represent two of them. Schrödinger had convinced himself that his waves could be something real, and not merely a probability distribution, but he could not persuade the rest. At the end of his presentation, Heisenberg indulged himself with the remark: "Herr Schrödinger trusts he will be capable of explaining and comprehending in three dimensions the results arising from his multidimensional theory once our knowledge has progressed further. I see nothing in his calculations to justify such a hope."

That afternoon, Heisenberg and Bohr presented their vision of quantum mechanics, which would come to be known as the Copenhagen Interpretation.

Reality, they said to those present, does not exist as something separate from the act of observation. A quantum object has no intrinsic properties. An electron is not in any fixed place until it is measured; it is only in that instant that it appears. Before being measured, it has no attributes; prior to observation, it cannot even be conceived of. It exists in a specific manner when it is detected by a specific instrument. Between one measurement and the next, there is no point in asking how it moves, what it is, or where it is located. Like the moon in Buddhism, a particle does not exist: it is the act of measuring that makes it a real object.

What they were proposing was a ruthless rupture with tradition. Physics ought not to concern itself with reality, but rather with what we can say about reality, they said. The being of atoms and their elementary particles was not like that of the objects of everyday experience. They live in worlds of potentialities, Heisenberg explained; they are not things, but possibilities. The transition from the "possible" to the "real" only occurred during the act of observation or measurement. There was, therefore, no independently existing quantum reality. Measured as a wave, an electron appeared as such; measured as a particle, it adopted this other form.

And then they went further.

None of these limits were theoretical: they were not a failure in the model, an experimental limitation or a technical difficulty. There simply existed no "real world" outside that science was capable of studying. "When we speak of the science of our era," Heisenberg explained, "we are talking about our relationship with nature, not as objective, detached observers, but as actors in a game between man and the world. Science can no longer confront reality in the same way. The method of analysing, explaining and classifying the world has become conscious of its own limitations: these arise from the fact that its interventions alter the objects it proposes to investigate. The light science shines on the world not only changes our vision of reality, but even the behaviour of its fundamental building blocks." Scientific method and its object could no longer be prised apart.

The proponents of the Copenhagen Interpretation concluded their lecture with a peremptory verdict: "We consider quantum mechanics to be a closed theory. Its underlying physics and mathematics are no longer amenable to modification."

This was more than Einstein could bear.

The iconoclast physicist par excellence refused to accept such a radical change. That physics should cease to speak of an objective world was not only a change in its point of view—it was a betrayal of the very spirit of science. For Einstein, physics *must* speak of causes and effects, and not only of probabilities. He refused to believe that the facts of the world obeyed a logic so contrary to common sense. Chance could not be enthroned at the expense of the notion of natural laws. There had to be something deeper. Something not yet known. A hidden variable that could dissipate the fog of Copenhagen and reveal the order that undergirded the randomness of the subatomic world. He was convinced of this, and over the next three days proposed a series of hypothetical situations that seemed to violate Heisenberg's uncertainty principle, which was the basis of the Copenhagen physicists' reasoning.

Every morning at breakfast—mirroring the official debates—Einstein would proffer his riddles, and every night Bohr would arrive with a solution. The duel between the two men dominated the conference, and divided the physicists into two opposing camps, but, in the end, Einstein had to yield. He had not found a single inconsistency in Bohr's reasoning. He accepted defeat grudgingly, and condensed all his hatred of quantum mechanics in a phrase he would repeat time and again in the succeeding years, one he practically spat in the Dane's face before his departure:

"God does not play dice with the universe!"

Epilogue

Einstein returned from Brussels to Paris with de Broglie. When he got off the train, he embraced him and told him not to despair, and to continue developing his ideas; there was no doubt he was on the right path. But de Broglie had lost something during those five days. Although he received the Nobel Prize in 1929 for his doctoral dissertation on matter waves, he capitulated to Heisenberg and Bohr's vision, and spent the rest of his career as a simple university professor, cut off from everyone by a kind of veil, a shame that served as a barrier between him and the world, one not even his sister managed to lift.

Einstein became the greatest enemy of quantum mechanics. He made countless efforts to find a way back to an objective world, searching for a hidden order that would unify his relativity theory and quantum mechanics and manage to uproot the chaos that had infected the most exact of all sciences. "This theory reminds me a little of the system of delusions of an exceedingly intelligent paranoiac, concocted of incoherent elements of thoughts," he wrote to one of his friends. He struggled to arrive at a grand unified theory and died without achieving it, admired by all, but completely alienated from the younger generations, who seemed to have accepted as definitive Bohr's response to Einstein at Solvay decades before, when he heard his sniping remark about God and dice: "It's not our place to tell Him how to run the world."

Schrödinger too came to detest quantum mechanics. He contrived an elaborate thought experiment, a *Gedankenexperiment*, the result of which was an apparently impossible creature: a cat that was, at once, alive and dead. His intention was to demonstrate the ridiculous character of this manner of thinking. The proponents of the Copenhagen Interpretation told Schrödinger that he was absolutely right: the result was not only ridiculous, but paradoxical. And yet it was true. Schrödinger's cat, like any elementary particle, was alive and dead (at least until it was measured), and the Austrian's name would remain associated forever with this failed attempt to negate the ideas he himself had helped give rise to. Schrödinger made contributions to biology, genetics, thermodynamics and general relativity, but never again produced anything comparable to what he had done during the six months following his stay in Villa Herwig, nor did he ever return there.

Fame accompanied him until his death in January 1961 at the age of seventy-three from a final attack of tuberculosis that besieged him in Vienna.

His equation remains a pillar of modern physics, though in a hundred years nobody has been able to unravel the mystery of the wave function.

Heisenberg was made a professor at the University of Leipzig at twenty-five—the youngest professor in the history of Germany. In 1932 he received the Nobel Prize for the creation of quantum mechanics, and in 1939 the Nazi government ordered him to investigate the feasibility of constructing a nuclear bomb; after two years, he concluded that a weapon of this type lay beyond the reach of Germany or any of its enemies, at least for the duration of the war, and he could hardly believe the news of the explosion over the sky of Hiroshima.

Heisenberg continued to develop provocative ideas for the rest of his life, and is considered one of the most important physicists of the twentieth century.

His uncertainty principle has never been disproved.

The Night
Gardener

I.

It is a vegetable plague, spreading from tree to tree. Unstoppable, invisible, a hidden rot, unseeing, unseen by the eyes of the world. Was it born of the deep dark earth? Was it brought to the surface by the mouths of the tiniest creatures? A fungus, perhaps? No, it travels faster than spores, it breeds inside tree roots, buried in their wooden hearts. An ancient, crawling evil. Kill it. Kill it with fire. Light it up and watch it burn, torch all those sickly beeches, firs and giant oaks that have stood the test of time, douse their trunks wounded from a thousand insect bites. Dying now, diseased and dying, dead as they stand. Let it burn and watch the flames reach up to the sky, for left alone it will consume the world, feeding on the death of others, nurtured by all the green grass turned grey. Quiet now, listen. Listen to it grow.

II.

I met him in the mountains, in a small town where few people live save during the summer months. I was walking at night and I saw him, in his garden, digging. My dog crawled under the bushes, ran towards him in the dark, a short white flash in the moonlight. The man bent over, rubbed her head, went down on one knee as my dog offered her belly. I apologized, he said it was OK, that he loved dogs. I asked him if he was gardening at night. "Yes," he said, "it's the best time for it. The plants are asleep and they don't feel as much, suffer less when moved around, like a patient etherized. We should be wary of plants." When he was a boy, there was a giant oak of which he had always been afraid. His grandmother hanged herself from one of its branches. Back then, he told me, it had been a healthy tree, strong and vigorous, while now, some sixty years later, its huge bulk was ridden with parasites and rotting from the inside, so much so that he knew that it would soon have to be removed, as it towered above his house and threatened to crush it if it came down. And yet he could not bring himself to fell the gargantuan thing, for it was one of the few remaining specimens of what used to be an old-growth forest that covered the land where his house and the whole town now stood, dark, foreboding and beautiful. He pointed at the tree, but in the dark I could see nothing save its massive shadow.

It was half dead, he said, rotten, yet still alive and growing. Bats nested inside its trunk and hummingbirds fed on the ruby red flowers of the parasitic plant which crowned its highest branches, the hermaphrodite *Tristerix corymbosus*, known locally as *quintral*, *cutre* or *ñipe*, which his grandmother used to cut back every year, only to see it regrow with stronger, denser blooms. "Why she killed herself I still don't know. They never told me she had committed suicide, it was a family secret, I was young, no more than five or six at the time, but later, decades later, when my daughter was born, my *nana*, my nanny, the woman who raised me while my own mother went to work, told me. 'Your grandmother,' she said, 'she hanged herself from that branch at night. It was awful, *terrible*, we could not cut her down till the police arrived, at least that is what they told us—"Don't cut her down, leave her there"— but your father could not leave her hanging like that, he climbed the tree, higher and higher— no one understood how she had climbed so high—and removed the noose from her neck. She fell through the branches, landed with a thud. Your father started hacking away at the trunk with his axe, but his father, your granddaddy, would not let him. He said that she had loved that tree, she always had. She had seen it grow, tended and nurtured it, pruned and watered it, and fussed over every tiny detail. So it stayed there and it's still here, though it's going to have to come down, sooner rather than later.'"

III.

The next morning I went for a walk in the woods with my seven-year-old daughter and we found the bodies of two dead dogs. They had been poisoned. I have never seen anything like it. I knew the bloodied corpses of puppies on the highway, crushed by tires of unrelenting traffic, I had seen a dead cat disembowelled by a pack of stray dogs, and I even stabbed the neck of an unsuspecting lamb myself and saw her bleed to death in front of the gauchos that I was staying with, who would roast her for an *asado*, but none of those deaths, however gruesome, came anywhere near the effects of poison. The first dog was a German shepherd, lying in the middle of the forest path. His mouth gaping, gums swollen and blackened, tongue out, five times its normal size, blood vessels filled to bursting point. I inched towards it and told my little girl to look away, but she would not listen and crept up behind me, burying her face in the folds of my jacket and peeking out. The dog's legs were stiff and stuck straight out, his abdomen had bloated with gases that stretched his skin and made it look like the belly of a pregnant woman. The whole cadaver seemed ready to explode and spill its entrails all over the place, but what struck me most was the expression of unrelenting pain on his features. Such was the agony he had endured that even in death he appeared to be screaming. The second dog was some fifty yards away, to the side of the trail, hidden in the undergrowth. It was a mongrel cross between a bloodhound and a beagle, with a black head on a white body, and even though he had surely died from the same substance that had killed the shepherd, he had suffered none of the disfiguring effects of the poison. Were it not for the flies crawling round his eyelids, I could have imagined he had merely fallen asleep. We did not know the first dog, but the hound was a friend of ours; my daughter had played with him since she was four, he would sometimes walk with us or come scratching at my door for scraps. She called him Patches and while she did not cry as soon as she recognized him, when we stepped out of the forest path and into the clearing, she broke down. I hugged her as hard as I could. She said she was afraid—as I was—for her own dog, the sweetest, kindest animal I have ever met. Why, she asked me, why were they poisoned? I told her I didn't know, but it was probably an accident; rat poison, slug poison, there are many deadly chemicals used for gardening, and there are many wonderful gardens in this place. They had probably eaten some poison without realizing what it was, or perhaps they had hunted a rat that was itself sluggish after chewing on those tiny wax cubes that people place around the borders of their properties. What I did not tell her is that this happens every year. Once or twice a year, dead dogs. Sometimes one, sometimes a lot more, but, unfailingly, the beginning of summer and the end of autumn bring dead dogs. The people who live here year round know that it is one of them who does the poisoning, one of their own, but no one knows who. He or she puts out cyanide, and for a couple of weeks we find carcasses around town. Strays, mostly, since lots of people from the neighbouring areas come up the mountain road to get rid of their unwanted dogs, but also our pets. There are a couple of suspects, individuals who have made threats in the past. There is a man who lives in the same street as we do, who once told a friend of mine that I should keep my dog on a lead. Did I not know that someone was poisoning dogs every summer? That man lives three houses down from ours, but I have never talked to him, and have only seen him once or twice, standing next to his car, smoking. He nods, I nod, but we do not talk.

IV.

I despair at how slowly my garden grows. The winters up in the mountain are harsh, spring and summer are short and very dry, and the soil in my garden is poor, as it was built on a rubbish heap. The former owner, the man who built the cabin and sold it to me, had to even out the terrain with rubble and construction debris, so that every now and then, when I dig into the ground to plant flowers and trees, I find cans, bottle caps and pieces of shredded plastic beneath the ground. There are a great number of fertilizers I could use, but I am fond of my trees as they are, even if they do not grow tall. Their roots have nowhere to go; below the thin layer of soil I have managed to pile over the rubbish lies hard, compact clay, so most will remain stunted, with a strange bonsai beauty, but stunted nonetheless. The night gardener told me that the man who invented modern-day nitrogen fertilizers—a German chemist called Fritz Haber—was also the first man to create a weapon of mass destruction, namely chlorine gas, which he poured into the trenches of the First World War. His green gas killed thousands and made countless soldiers claw at their throats as the poison boiled inside their lungs, drowning them in their own vomit and phlegm, while his fertilizer, which he harvested from the nitrogen present in the air itself, saved hundreds of millions from famine and fuelled our current overpopulation. Today nitrogen is more than plentiful, but in centuries past wars were fought over bird and bat shit, and thieves ransacked the bones of the Egyptian pharaohs to steal the nitrogen hidden in their bones. According to the night gardener, the Mapuche Indians would crush the skeletons of their vanquished enemies and spread that dust on their farms as fertilizer, always working in the dead of night, when the trees are fast asleep, for they believed that some of them—the *canelo* and the *araucaria*, the monkey puzzle—could see into a warrior's soul, steal his deepest secrets and spread them through the shared roots of the forest, where plush tendrils whispered to pale mushroom mycelium, ruining his standing before the community. His secret life lost, exposed and bared to the world, the man would slowly begin to shrivel, drying up from the inside out, without ever knowing why.

V.

The way this small town is built is very strange. Whichever road you take, it will invariably lead you down to a small patch of woods tucked away at its lowest edge, one of the few areas that survived the giant fire which ravaged the region at the end of the Nineties, threatening the existence of the town itself. The fire raged until it burned itself out. A forest that had stood for two hundred years disappeared in less than two weeks. It was mostly replanted with pine, and the original, native species were all lost, except for this tiny miniature wilderness, which stands in stark contrast to the pruned hedges and decorative gardens that surround it on all sides. It has a strange magnetic power over me, it pulls me in and leads me down and down towards the old path that reaches the lake. I have spent days walking among the trees there, always alone, for the locals seem to avoid the area, although I do not know why, and most outsiders, the rich families who rent cottages for the summer months, visit it rarely, or only see it in passing. There is a small grotto at its centre, carved in limestone. The night gardener tells me there used to be a giant plant nursery that kept its seeds inside the mouth of the cave, in perpetual darkness. It is empty these days, visited now and then by adolescent boys and girls who leave their condom wrappers on the ground or tourists whose soiled toilet paper I have to pick up and bury.

The lake lies beyond, and that small stretch of water is where families gather. It is artificial, man-made, more a pond than a lake really, but it looks natural enough for a dozen ducks to nest there. A red-tailed hawk patrols the southern side; a white crane lords over the northern, swampier half. In spring the tiny streams that feed the reservoir trickle and sing, but later they dry up, are overgrown and disappear as if they had never existed. The lake has not frozen over in decades. I was told that a small child drowned after falling through the ice the last time it did, back when Pinochet had just come to power, but no one has been able to tell me the little boy's name. It's probably just a tale to keep the children away from the lake at night, one that has survived even though the climate has warmed and ice no longer forms.

This town was founded by European immigrants. There is a decidedly foreign feel to this place, one that is not common in other parts of Chile, even though there are some small southern cities where you can also see blonde blue-eyed girls running among our decidedly homogenous mix of Spaniards and Mapuches. This place was built as a haven, high up in the mountains. One of the things that has always surprised me about Chile is that we do not inhabit the mountains. The Andes are there like a sword stuck down our backs, but we ignore those fabulous peaks and settle on the coast, as if the whole country suffered from terminal vertigo, a fear of heights that stops us from enjoying the most prominent feature of our unique landscape. Less than an hour away from this town, right where you leave the highway to head up the mountain road, there is a huge military garrison; the house I bought was built by a retired army lieutenant. I did a little research on him out of curiosity, and saw that he was accused of being involved in the disappearance of several political prisoners during the dictatorship. I met him on only two occasions: when he showed me the place and when we signed the papers. I did not know at the time, though I suspected it because of the low price he asked, but he was terminally ill. He died less than a year later. The night gardener tells me he was a hateful man, despised by everyone in town, since he would walk around with his old service revolver at his hip and refuse to pay workers for the repairs they did to his house. When we moved in, I found an old grenade atop one of the coffee tables in the living room, with no firing pin. Try as I might, I cannot remember what I did with it.

VI.

The night gardener used to be a mathematician, and now speaks of mathematics as former alcoholics speak of booze, with a mixture of fear and longing. He told me that he had had the beginnings of a brilliant career but had quit altogether after encountering the work of Alexander Grothendieck, a world-famous mathematician who revolutionized geometry as no one had since the time of Euclid, and who inexplicably gave up mathematics at the height of his international fame, leaving a bewildering legacy that is still sending shock waves through all branches of his discipline, but which he completely refused to discuss, right up to his death in 2014. Like the night gardener, when Grothendieck turned forty, he left his house, his family and his friends, and lived like a monk, holed up in the Pyrenees. It was as if Einstein had given up physics after publishing his theory of relativity, or Maradona had decided never to touch a ball after winning the World Cup. The night gardener's decision to drop out of life was not merely because of his admiration for Grothendieck, of course. He had also gone through a bad divorce, become estranged from his only daughter and been diagnosed with skin cancer, but he insisted that all of that, however painful, was secondary to the sudden realization that it was mathematics—not nuclear weapons, computers, biological warfare or our climate

Armageddon—which was changing our world to the point where, in a couple of decades at most, we would simply not be able to grasp what being human really meant. Not that we ever did, he said, but things are getting worse. We can pull atoms apart, peer back at the first light and predict the end of the universe with just a handful of equations, squiggly lines and arcane symbols that normal people cannot fathom, even though they hold sway over their lives. But it's not just regular folks; even scientists no longer comprehend the world. Take quantum mechanics, the crown jewel of our species, the most accurate, far-ranging and beautiful of all our physical theories. It lies behind the supremacy of our smartphones, behind the Internet, behind the coming promise of godlike computing power. It has completely reshaped our world. We know how to use it, it works as if by some strange miracle, and yet there is not a human soul, alive or dead, who actually gets it. The mind cannot come to grips with its paradoxes and contradictions. It's as if the theory had fallen to earth from another planet, and we simply scamper around it like apes, toying and playing with it, but with no true understanding.

So he gardens now, tends to his own and also works on other properties in town. He has no friends that I know of, and his few neighbours consider him a bit of a weirdo, but I like to think of him as my friend as he will sometimes leave buckets of compost outside my house, as a gift for my garden. The oldest tree on my property is a lemon, a sprawling mass of twigs with a heavy bow. The night gardener once asked me if I knew how citrus trees died: when they reach old age, if they are not cut down and they manage to survive drought, disease and innumerable attacks of pests, fungi and plagues, they succumb from overabundance. When they come to the end of their life cycle, they put out a final, massive crop of lemons. In their last spring their flowers bud and blossom in enormous bunches and fill the air with a smell so sweet that it stings your nostrils from two blocks away; then their fruits ripen all at once, whole limbs break off due to their excessive weight, and after a few weeks the ground is covered with rotting lemons. It is a strange sight, he said, to see such exuberance before death. One can picture it in animal species, those million salmon mating and spawning before dropping dead, or the billions of herrings that turn the seawater white with their sperm and eggs and cover the coasts of the northeast Pacific for hundreds of miles. But trees are very different organisms, and such displays of overripening feel out of character for a plant and more akin to our own species, with its uncontrolled, devastating growth. I asked him how long my own citrus had to live. He told me that there was no way to know, at least not without cutting it down and looking inside its trunk. But, really, who would want to do that?

Acknowledgements

I would like to thank Constanza Martínez for her invaluable contribution to this book, namely for her fighting with me over every little detail. This is a work of fiction based on real events. The quantity of fiction grows throughout the book; whereas "Prussian Blue" contains only one fictional paragraph, I have taken greater liberties in the subsequent texts, while still trying to remain faithful to the scientific concepts discussed in each of them. The case of Shinichi Mochizuki, one of the protagonists of "The Heart of the Heart," is a peculiar one: I did take inspiration from certain aspects of his work to enter into the mind of Alexander Grothendieck, but most of what is said here about him, his biography, and his research is fiction. The majority of historical and biographical references employed in the book can be found in the following books and articles, whose authors I would also like to thank, although a complete list would be excessively long: Walter Moore, *Schrödinger: Life and Thought*; Manjit Kumar, *Quantum: Einstein, Bohr and the Great Debate About the Nature of Reality*; Christianus Democritus, *Maladies and Remedies of the Life of the Flesh*; John Gribbin, *Erwin Schrödinger and the Quantum Revolution*; Erwin Schrödinger, *My View of the World*; Alexander Grothendieck, *Récoltes et Semailles*; Arthur I. Miller, *Erotica, Aesthetics and Schrödinger's Wave Equation*; Werner Heisenberg, *Physics and Philosophy: The Revolution in Modern Science*; David Lindley, *Uncertainty: Einstein, Heisenberg, Bohr and the Struggle for the Soul of Science*; Winfried Scharlau and Melissa Schneps (trans.), *Who Is Alexander Grothendieck? Anarchy, Mathematics, Spirituality, Solitude*; Ian Kershaw, *Hitler*; W.G. Sebald, *The Rings of Saturn*; Karl Schwarzschild, *Collected Works*; Jeremy Bernstein, *The Reluctant Father of Black Holes*.

Benjamín Labatut was born in Rotterdam in 1980 and grew up in The Hague, Buenos Aires and Lima. He has published two award-winning works of fiction prior to *When We Cease to Understand the World*, which is his first book to be translated into English. Labatut lives with his family in Santiago, Chile.

Adrian Nathan West is a writer, critic, and literary translator based in Spain. He is author of *The Aesthetics of Degradation* and the forthcoming *My Father's Diet* and *The Philosophy of a Visit*. His translations include works by Sibylle Lacan, Hermann Burger, and Mario Vargas Llosa.